Dedication

For John.

Acknowledgement

BWL Publishing acknowledges the Province of Alberta for their ongoing support through the Alberta Publisher's Cultural Industry Operating Grant.

Table of Contents

Chapter 1

Grant was late.

Jodi knew, because her heating pad had automatically turned off.

Turning it on was a part of her morning routine. Make a cup of creamy coffee, unlock her basement suite door, sit at her editing computer, and flick on the heating pad at her back. A few minutes later, Grant—squat, sunburnt Grant, with his grey, bead-adorned rattail flying behind him—would burst into the room and announce, like a newscaster, some disaster that had befallen him somewhere between his house and hers. Once, a pig had darted across the street, bamboozling traffic. Another time, he'd been pulled over for resembling a convict who'd escaped the local prison, and had nearly been arrested for being cheeky.

That had been his word. *Cheeky.* Jodi suspected he'd done more than be *cheeky,* but she said nothing. Despite his boisterous nature, the fifty-something man she edited camping videos for took easy offence at any suggestion of wrongdoing. She'd once made the light suggestion that he clean his camera lens, and he'd not contacted her for two weeks.

She couldn't afford to lose him as a client. He singlehandedly kept her rent paid. So even if he demanded she throw away her air fresheners and incense—he hated smells, and Jodi's nose didn't work very well—even if he drank all her lychee drinks, even if he suggested she pause her time clock whenever he started some long-winded story because he knew she'd get "a kick out of it," she went along gladly. He wasn't a bad guy. She liked him. Even if he was completely insane.

The one thing she did not like was his lack of punctuality. He was normally a few minutes late, but he sometimes took longer. Often it was when he reached the event horizon of a daily disaster and was unable to escape.

It wasn't missing a session that bothered Jodi—it wasn't, after all, Grant's fault a murder of crows descended upon his green bins and scattered a weekly collection of edamame husks over a fifty-foot stretch of sidewalk—it was that he failed, every time, to call her about it.

He owned a phone. She'd seen it, many times, when it made a noise and he pulled it from his pocket with a baffled expression, as though the thing had appeared from thin air. Then he'd give a happy little scoff and slide it back into his pocket, and Jodi couldn't help but imagine her own calls getting the same brush-off.

An hour was her limit. After that, she could count on a free afternoon. Unless he called several hours later with a hearty sigh and a "Well, I suppose it'll be an evening session," as though Jodi's video editing service kept the hours of an all-night bistro.

It would be worse, she supposed, if she used her time well. If she went out regularly. Or often.

Or sometimes.

At all.

The trouble was, today was a different day. She *was* going out.

On a date.

Her first date in two years.

Her mother had found the girl. "She's the instructor of my Zumba class." Her mother's tone was proud. "I'm telling you, she's not into all that online nonsense. She lives in the moment. You'll love her, Jodi."

"We'll see."

There was a tinge of nervousness to her mother's reply. "You can't be picky, Jodi."

Taking her mother's relationship advice was not something Jodi loved doing. However, she'd been worn down. Jodi wasn't a relationship expert, either.

It was a shame Grant had chosen today to miss a session; Jodi had been looking forward to telling him about her date. No session was complete without him giving the room a cursory glance and shaking his head dramatically, a callback to a conversation when he'd hired her. At their first session, Jodi had recently become single, and her apartment showed it. Grant had been a half hour early and caught her lethargically shoving drink cans and food wrappers into a garbage bag.

"If ever anyone needed a wife," he'd said.

Jodi, not knowing whether to laugh or cry, settled on a tired, "Yeah."

His eyes had fallen on the square of missing drywall behind her workstation. "And a husband."

She didn't see Grant as a father figure. He was too self-absorbed, too unpredictable. His words of wisdom were few and far between, and usually tipped left on a scale of chaos to sense. He'd once exited Jodi's bathroom holding out her toothbrush as though it were cursed. "Smart girl like you should realize you don't need this hoohah. Did you know that other cultures just use a stick?"

Jodi wished he wouldn't carry her toothbrush by the head. "A specific kind, yes."

Grant shook his head, waggling the toothbrush like a conductor. "It's just a stick."

"No, it's a soft, bristly kind from a specific tree...have you just been using any stick?"

Grant ran his tongue across his teeth, and Jodi noticed just how red his gums were.

He'd been distinctly cool to her for the rest of the session.

He wasn't a father figure, but she still wanted him to know she'd found herself a date.

* * *

Jodi was laughing. She was with a stranger, and she was laughing. There were snorts even, which was embarrassing, but not too much.

Perhaps *stranger* wasn't accurate anymore, either. The woman's name was Evelyn, her cinnamon eyes sparkled, and a smile never left her sunshiny face. Jodi had found it disarming at first, but it became charming as the night evolved. There were little lines already forming where Evelyn's smile creased her face—a good sign.

Evelyn had big reactions. Perhaps they were exaggerated—Jodi didn't feel her own bachelor's degree deserved an exclaimed "Amazing!"—but Jodi didn't care. The woman was listening, and she was nice, and it had been far too long since a nice person listened to Jodi talk.

Jodi didn't even mind that her date had chosen the most expensive restaurant in the city—Jodi assumed it was, anyway, having choked on her spit when she'd read the menu. Though it was possible inflation had been dramatic in the two years Jodi had avoided restaurants.

Evelyn didn't seem the type to expect a free meal—more the type to throw down her credit card with a smile. The refusal was sitting prepared on Jodi's tongue, despite her purse straps struggling under the weight of toonie rolls she'd scavenged from her emergency piggy bank in an effort to avoid her abused credit card, and her fear it wouldn't be enough.

Stop it. You'll regret missing out on a great girl more than missing a credit card payment.

The longer they ate and talked and drank, the more it sank in. Jodi was really doing this. After two years, she was getting back into the game. Finally.

Evelyn, an asparagus spear sticking out her mouth like a cigar, pulled out her phone and checked it. "My friend is wondering how things are going."

"Did you have a failsafe? In case I turned out to be a nutjob?" The wine was making Jodi confident and flirty.

Evelyn gave Jodi a coy look. "Spontaneous labour. Two weeks early. It would've been very dramatic." Suddenly, her phone was up, camera facing Jodi. "Smile!"

Jodi tried, but couldn't quite manage anything authentic. Her flirtatiousness had left out the side door. "What are you doing?"

"Making her jealous. She's elevating her cankles and I'm having dinner with a gorgeous video editor."

Instantly, Jodi's face flamed, and she was still struggling for a clever reply as Evelyn tapped away at her phone, sending the photo of Jodi to her friend. Desperately, Jodi stuck the straw in her mouth and drank like she was dying.

"So." Evelyn placed her phone on the table and laced her fingers under her chin. "What's your main goal in life?"

Jodi's straw fell back into the glass with a tiny *tink*. "To get through it in one piece."

Evelyn smiled her big smile, and Jodi knew her answer wasn't good enough. It was a non-answer.

She tried to think of something less whiny and trite. "But another big one is finding someone to share it with."

Yikes. This was worse. And it wasn't entirely true...but it was partly true. And shouldn't you be partly true on a date?

Yes, idiot, but not to the point of being cringy and creepy. Her flirtiness was not returning for the second act, and for the first time, Jodi wished her date was less smiley. It was way too difficult to translate the good smiles from the bad. *This woman could walk beaming into an iron maiden.*

"I think that's a great goal." The smile didn't waver. "Life can be pretty dull without someone to share it with."

Dull wasn't a bad word, to Jodi. "It's also, like..." She thought about it. "I'd like a life of sharing those dull bits. I want a home with tons of couches and recliners, except I'd still rather squeeze next to my partner on a tiny couch to read." Jodi cleared her throat and twirled some pasta on her fork. "But to be more realistic, I'd love to continue school. Go to some big, old school in Europe, where I can edit remotely and work on a super useless PhD."

"In what?"

"Not sure. As long as I can be called doctor and still be useless on a plane, I'm happy." Jodi wondered if that sounded stupid. "Is that a bad goal?"

Evelyn shook her head. "Imagine the stress medical doctors feel on planes. Always on call." Evelyn's phone buzzed, and she took a quick glance.

And there—there it was.

The barest twitch in the corners of her smile.

At the same time, Evelyn's eyes flashed up to Jodi's face, then back down to her phone.

If Jodi had not spent the last hour gazing at that unmoving smile, she'd never have noticed. But she had. And she did.

It was quick. It'd be a couple frames in a video. Jodi could've cut it out—that 1/12 of a second, with the eyes flashing shocked recognition and mouth twitching with disgust—and no one would've noticed the skip.

And just like that, the familiar feeling in her gut. Like she'd snake-swallowed the toonie rolls in her bag and wandered onto an enormous magnet.

Evelyn slid the phone into her fanny pack and took another bite of asparagus, eyes flitting around the room. "I'm just going to pop off to the bathroom." She stood and covertly wound her jacket around her arm as she pushed her chair in.

"Water broke?"

Evelyn's mouth popped open, and her gaze flicked down to her jacket while she struggled visibly for an explanation. In the end she simply turned and wound around the tables, head down.

"Wish you didn't order steak." The words came out a lot louder than Jodi'd intended, and just as the waiter appeared— as if by inconvenient magic—at her table. He had on a pair of confidently ostentatious yellow glasses and a frown that did nothing to hide his bubbling desire to run to the back and tell the staff about this newest drama. "And how are things going?"

"Good." Jodi pushed away her half-eaten chicken parmesan.

"Stunning. Stunning. We just ask that we keep voices down." He gestured with both hands, as though giving slow and ineffective CPR. "We don't want to bother other guests."

"I said one thing loud. I'll shut up now."

"Stunning. How was your chicken parm?"

"Best I've had today. Listen—" Jodi dropped her voice. "Is it possible to just pay for my own meal?" With pleading eyes she held up her purse, as though he could see how empty her bank account was, or at least the rolls of desperate toonies at the bottom.

His eyes flicked to the plate across the table, then he gave her a sympathetic smile. "I'm afraid you'll have to pay for the meals you've eaten."

"I didn't eat that one, though. Can't you, you know..." Jodi mimed something with her arms helplessly. "Go and tackle her or something?"

"No, I'm so sorry, we aren't allowed to tackle customers."

"She'd only be a customer if she paid."

"We aren't allowed to tackle non-customers, either."

Jodi nodded and looked in her purse, at the rolled-up toonies. "I'll need the machine."

"Stunning."

He turned on his heel and beelined for the back. Jodi watched until he disappeared, then placed a single roll of toonies next to her plate. Enough to pay for her own cheapish meal, but not the half-eaten cut of expensive beef on the abandoned plate across the table.

She didn't want to do it. She felt dirty and scummy. But mainly, she felt broke.

So she stood and, with casual speed, headed for the exit, the weight of patrons' eyes on her. Despite what the waiter had said, she was fully braced for impact, and was somewhat shocked when the cold air hit her face outside. That was when she ran, like the food-stealing criminal she was. *And I'm not even full.*

A helicopter buzzed low overhead. Though she knew police were unlikely to respond to a dine-and-dash, and even less likely to charter a helicopter to find the culprit, Jodi urged her legs faster.

* * *

For the rest of that evening, Jodi waited for Grant to call and reschedule, though she didn't have high hopes. He'd likely forgotten to mention a hot tent trip at their last session, and of course he'd never call or email.

Jodi knew what she was in this man's life. An appliance. Like an air fryer. He liked her, and he'd say good things about her, and certainly used her when convenient, but he'd never courtesy call an air fryer.

Jodi lay on her couch and listened to the sound of the night. From a vent leading to the upstairs living room, she heard the thumping footsteps and muffled exhales of her elderly landlord, Mr. Doucette, on his ancient treadmill. He worked out late at night, often when Jodi was just falling asleep, on the rare days he didn't start right before Jodi's 7AM alarm.

She didn't mind. He didn't use his key to snoop in her suite, and didn't mind if, sometimes, her rent came in toonies.

She checked her phone and saw that she'd gotten a couple emails. One was from a university in Scotland, answering her inquiry about their master's program. The other was a comment on an account she'd still not deactivated.

Kill yourself.

She deleted it. Like all the others.

Chapter 2

"Doesn't it rain enough so you don't have to do this?"

Jodi's next-door neighbour, Harper, scoffed as she swept the spray of water across the massive expanse of dirt before them. Harper's straight blond hair was wrapped up in a hasty knot and, unwilling to dirty the massive mint-coloured cloak she often wore, she'd thrown on her husband Evan's puffer jacket and hiking boots, which dwarfed her short frame. "Unless it's constant, it's not going to work. Are you going to help me?"

"How?" Jodi wrapped her worn, blue-plaid mackinaw tighter around herself and curled smaller into the dirty Adirondack chair. "My knuckles hurt."

"My knuckles don't have feeling at all. Come on, take it." Harper pressed the cold, wet hose into Jodi's unwilling hand. "This is as much for you as it is for me."

This was about ten percent true. In late spring, when the two of them moved their Colt 45 drinking sessions from the kitchen table to the barely sun-warmed patio, Jodi had made a singular comment about how nice it would be if Harper's lawn wasn't made of molehills and weeds. Since then, Harper's ferocious remodelling of her entire yard—a process that took most of the summer and well into the fall—was *for Jodi.* It would have been a nice sentiment, if *for Jodi* meant it was a gift and not a lovechild that required co-parenting.

Jodi cringed as freezing water leaked from the hose and over her aching hand. Behind her came the sound of violent stomping.

"These." *Stomp.* "Stupid." *Stomp.* "Frigging." *Stomp.* "Moles." *Stomp.* Harper spat a piece of hair out of her mouth. "The meat was probably bad."

"Mole meat? Yeah, probably."

"I meant the dinner. With that girl. Maybe she went to puke."

It had been a week and a half since Jodi's horrible date. Since then, Harper—not only Jodi's neighbour, but her sole friend—had come up with every excuse in the book to explain Evelyn's departure. Her musings came between her lectures on how the date had been a bad idea from the start—*"You're still a mess. You're about as ready to date as my husband is ready to accept that pickleball is ping pong for people who want to walk a little. I don't know what your mum was thinking."*

The thing was, Jodi agreed with her friend. She *wasn't* ready for a relationship, and had gone on a date mainly for her mother's sake. Still, while at first Jodi was grateful for Harper's optimism regarding bad meat, Jodi was more than ready to talk about anything else.

It didn't help that Jodi's backburner was already simmering with stress unrelated to her love life. Bills had wounded her chequing account badly, and Grant had not called to reschedule his missed session, nor the session he missed the following week. Jodi's other gigs kept her in lychee drinks and Kraft Dinner, but Grant was her cash cow who had, apparently, wandered out of the pasture. *Likely onto a freeway.*

Jodi had not told Harper about running out on the restaurant bill. Harper knew funds were tight with Jodi but didn't know how bad it was. It was embarrassing talking money with Harper, who never touched a toonie roll in her life. Unfortunately, embarrassment made Jodi shell out for pricy café coffee whenever Harper had the hankering—which was often. Yet, as much as Jodi couldn't afford the expense, she could afford even less appearing pathetic in front of the only person she saw these days.

Jodi shook herself out of the stress-trance and continued saturating the lawn. "I don't think this place would give you food poisoning. It was a cloth napkin joint. And I thought Evan set mole traps?"

"They don't work. It's because he *touched them.*" Harper shouted the last words at the house, then turned back to Jodi with an annoyed expression. "The person at Buckerfield's told us to use gloves, but Mister No-Ears up there wasn't listening. Now his stupid scent is all over the traps and the little assholes won't get near them." Harper tended to save all her irritation for when Jodi came over, at which point she'd unstopper it like a viciously shaken bottle of pop. Grumbling, Harper walked over to the spigot and turned off the water.

Jodi dropped the hose on the ground and wiped her frozen hand on her overalls. "I'm thinking of going to Scotland."

Harper's confused eyes rose to meet Jodi's. "What? Why?" She wound the hose.

"School. And just...because."

Harper shook her head as she hooked the hose on its hanger. "You're not doing it."

"How do you know?"

"You hate rain."

"I live in the rainiest city in Canada."

"Exactly. Why would you move somewhere worse?" Harper gestured to the grey sky. "Here, at least it stops raining long enough to kill my lawn."

"I thought it was *our* lawn."

"And what, you'd just lug your fifty-pound computer there?"

"It's just a thought."

Harper studied Jodi's face, then let out a sigh. "You can't run from your life."

"I can try."

"You're not leaving me alone." Harper gestured again. "Think of the *lawn*."

Harper could joke—she always did—but outside her mother and Harper, Jodi didn't feel any roots keeping her here. Her hometown was blighted two years ago. It was possible the peace she sought wasn't attainable in the musty suite with the yet-to-be-fixed hole in the drywall.

With the lawn finally watered, Jodi followed Harper into her blessedly warm kitchen. Harper chucked her mug in the sink, then was suddenly preoccupied with something outside the window. "You've got a weird-looking Jehovah's Witness at your door."

Jodi joined Harper at the window and peeked out at the neighbouring house. From here, they could see through the sparse hedge to the cement steps leading down to Jodi's suite.

Sitting on the steps was a person. They were doubled over, arms on their knees.

"Could be a tweaker." Jodi shot a desperate look at her friend. "Can Evan scare them off?"

"Evan sets the mole traps but forces me to check them. He's not your best bet for a bodyguard." Harper was forever unimpressed by her husband's lack of masculinity. Jodi often wondered if Harper liked her husband at all.

Stomach uneasy, Jodi left Harper's and headed through the hedge towards the stone steps. In her mind she rehearsed her plan of action. Asking if the person was okay was her instinctual first choice, but she'd taken enough public transit to know that asking about a weird stranger's wellbeing could lead to them pressing uncomfortably close on a near-empty bus and talking at length about their dead ex-wife, their recent prison sentence, and the unnervingly over-stated assurance that the two events weren't related.

And then there was the other possibility. The one that *really* scared her. The possibility that the invisible, anonymous viciousness from online had snuck into physical life.

By the time she reached the steps, she'd settled on simply ignoring the person, and stepping over them like she would a molehill.

But then, the person looked up, and they didn't look like a tweaker. Their wavy black hair had been styled at one point that day, though was out of place from the hunched position. The dark burgundy parka was ripless and the black jeans clean and wrinkle-free, though Jodi's mother would zero in on the tattoo peeking out from the collar and assume something was wrong. (Jodi had stated at least twenty times that tattoos weren't in her immediate future but was increasingly tempted the more her mother brought it up.)

Their face was...quite beautiful, to Jodi's astonishment. A once-in-a-blue-moon face. A   should-be-on-a-bus-ad-for-eyeglasses face. Perfectly curved largish nose, high cheekbones, intense brows. Skin like smooth ironwood, and eyes as dark as graphite—eyes that were currently sizing Jodi up with unsettling wariness.

Despite her previous plan, the instinctual words bubbled up. "Are you okay?"

"Are you Jodi?"

Jodi's stomach twisted as her mind flashed with gruesome possibilities, but the person didn't look angry. "Yes?"

With some difficulty, the person stood—they were much taller than Jodi expected. "I have a good reason to be here. But I have to make a really bad first impression." The person held up an empty takeaway cup. "Can I use your bathroom?"

Jodi spent several seconds staring at the cup. "Um."

The person stretched out a leg, as though urging their bowels to use the extra space. "I do not have time for you to be skeptical of me. I'm two seconds from shitting my pants."

Is this a new crime tactic?

"Jodi." The way the person said her name—the patronization of a teacher and the desperation of a hostage. "Either you open the door, or I'm digging a hole in your front yard."

As if in a trance, Jodi pulled her key from her pocket. Apparently, this wasn't enough, because before she could say or do a thing, the key was out of her hand and twisting in the lock. The person disappeared inside Jodi's house, and she was left frozen on the stoop, staring at the key left in the lock.

Part of her wanted to return to Harper's for help, but how would she explain herself? *"So I gave that tweaker and/or Jehovah's Witness my key, but in my defence, they're very good-looking..."*

No. Jodi was already a hot mess express. There were only so many pitying looks she could handle. So she pulled the key from the lock, took a steadying breath, and stepped into her apartment.

Immediately she was struck by how messy it was. Nothing by the intruder—Jodi had simply not been kept in check by her weekly visits from Grant. Without his shrewd eyes scanning the place, she'd stepped out of three pairs of pants without scooping them up and had let dishes overwhelm several surfaces, including—and the embarrassment overtook her fear at this recollection—her half-empty coffee mug sitting right on the back of the toilet.

There was the sound of a flush, then the crank of the old sink. Jodi fussed with her hands, wondering what expression to put on her face. Irritation? Fury? She felt like this was enough to call the police about, but she was also tempted to apologize for the state of her house, and somehow there was no middle ground to explore.

She'd just noticed how dusty her desk was when the door opened and the person exited, wiping wet hands on their jeans. Or, rather, wiping one wet hand. In the other was Jodi's toilet mug, which was silently held out for her to take.

"Oh, that's where that went." Jodi took it and placed it on the dusty desk.

The person's eyes followed its journey. "You don't have a sink?"

This judgement from the stranger who had broken into Jodi's house and crapped unwelcome in her toilet was the final straw. "Yes, I have a sink. In the laundry room, which I use as a kitchen."

"Want me to take it there?" The person's fingers twitched towards the mug.

Jodi snatched it up. "How about we head back outside?"

The person's eyes roamed Jodi's living room, landing on her computer. A hungry look passed over their face, and Jodi's veins ran cold. That computer was her only form of income.

Before Jodi could do a thing—*throw the mug?*—the person's eyes snapped back to Jodi. "Do you watch the news?"

"Why do you—"

Just then, a phone buzzed. The person pulled it from their pocket, checked it, then sped to the door. "Hello?" They pulled it open, went outside, and jogged up the cement steps.

Jodi unfroze and ran to the door. After whipping it closed, she secured the knob lock and security chain.

This wasn't enough, so Jodi sped to the door she almost never used; behind it were the stairs up to her landlord's apartment.

Jodi clomped up the stairs and knocked, praying Mr. Doucette was home. The man was in his eighties, but if his late-night/early-morning exercises were of any indication, he still had some fight in him.

The door opened, and he stuck his wispy head through the crack. "Toilet plugged?"

"Mr. Doucette, I'm so sorry, but can I sit in your apartment until this strange person leaves my front stoop?"

He narrowed his eyes—made huge by thick reading glasses—then pulled the door open all the way, sending a waft of strong lavender into Jodi's face. "I thought your toilet was plugged."

"No, it's fine."

"I heard it flush, then you came up here."

"That wasn't me." Jodi edged past Mr. Doucette and was struck by the apartment around her. In the corner was the infamous treadmill, and the floors and surfaces were stacked with boxes. On one nearest the door, scrawled with a Sharpie, was the label *Belle's nonsense*. A few were more passionately labelled with *Belle's horseshit* or *Belle's 58th box of crap*. It was as though he were just moving in. "Is Belle your…"

"Late wife. Had to empty a storage unit, the building got black mould." Mr. Doucette closed the door and locked it. "Was it that bizarre leprechaun who used to come here? Kept seeing him skulking around. Asked who he was, and he says I don't need to know. Almost hit him with my truck."

"That's just Grant, my client. Sorry—he's the type to walk into the road without looking."

"No, I almost hit him on purpose. Weird fucker. Didn't like the look of him. You shouldn't be hanging around weird old men, girl." He pulled a grey sock from his sweatpants pocket and let loose into it an explosive sneeze.

"Weird old men I'm okay with." Jodi peeked through his blinds. "But young people...they freak me out."

"Hmph."

"They can use the internet."

"Would you stop twisting my blinds, it takes me forever to get them sitting right. Look at that."

Jodi sheepishly watched Mr. Doucette stalk over and fiddle with the curtain panels, which she'd slightly off-set with her peeping. Then from downstairs came the sound of knocking, and Mr. Doucette immediately parted the curtains with two fingers to look outside. "Still out there. Did you do something to piss 'em off?"

"I don't think so." Jodi remembered what the person had said—that they had a good reason to be here. Still, people believed there was a good reason for anything.

"They took off."

"What?" Jodi jumped to look outside, but Mr. Doucette didn't budge from his lookout point.

"Got tired of standing around." He glanced back at Jodi. "I hope you don't have a cat."

"A cat?" Jodi blinked. "No. Why?"

"Not allowed one. It's on the lease."

"Have I given the impression I have a cat?" She paused. "Recently?"

He let out a cough into the sock. "It's the fifteenth."

Was it? Jodi winced. "Ah, yes—I—"

"I wouldn't mind all bills this time. I've got too many coins. You own a vending machine?"

Jodi backed to the door. The truth was, Grant made it a point to pay with anything but an e-transfer—sometimes it was a crumpled cheque, sometimes it was bills, sometimes it was rolls of coins. Jodi had turned the inconvenience into a budgeting tactic—they were too cumbersome to spend, so they were easy to save. "It might take a day or so."

Mr. Doucette gave her a searching look. Jodi grinned with as much charm as she possessed while backing to the door.

Jodi had no idea how far she could push Mr. Doucette. He could be a lenient man, or someone who'd evict her with little warning.

Instability scared her, yet she tended to attract the unstable, so she'd never pushed him far enough to find out. But she might have to, if Grant—a wobbly pillar of instability—had indeed moved on from his desire to make videos. His payment every session, be it bills, cheque, or coin rolls, was something she'd taken for granted.

In her suite, Jodi collapsed onto the worn carpet. She had made the critical error of becoming too dependant on an unpredictable man. But he'd been consistent for a year, with no signs of losing interest. His missed sessions were never due to his lack of desire, only his seeming inability to navigate life peril-free. He'd never missed two in a row before.

Without him, she wouldn't have enough to afford the suite. She needed more clients, or a different job altogether. If that failed, she'd have to ask her mother for a loan, if the money existed to borrow. Likely it didn't, and her mother would instead make the cheerful offer to move back home. *"I don't even know why you need that suite anymore in the first place. I just have to move Dad's stuff out of the spare room. You can help me go through it."*

Jodi shuddered as she grabbed her purse and upended it on the floor. She sorted through receipts and hair ties, searching for coins or tightly folded bills that may have escaped her wallet. Even four years post-move-out, Jodi's mother had yet to understand why Jodi left behind a life of free rent and companionship in a big, clean house. That instead she chose to live in a tiny, musty basement with no proper kitchen and the gaping drywall hole covered in plastic that gently rippled behind her as she worked. (Eventually, the drywallers would come. She hoped.)

Jodi couldn't explain it to her mother. That Jodi's father's life and death wrapped around that house, around her mother, and to return was a concept so exhausting that Jodi couldn't bear to think of it.

Among the debris of her bag wasn't any money, but she did unearth a card that she'd gotten during a pride event. It was for a local brewery. *One free flight on us.*

She searched for the expiration date. It expired in a week.

Beer has calories. That'd take care of a meal.

Jodi had planned on staying in that day, especially after her visitor. But the messy apartment wasn't doing her mental health any favours, so she pulled on her mackinaw and, very slowly, opened the door.

No one was there. Relieved, she pulled it open all the way and stepped out.

She was at the top of the concrete steps when she saw, with a jolt of irritation and fear, the person sitting on the ground, scrolling on their phone. On seeing her, they scrambled to their feet.

"I'm friends with my landlord," were the first words that popped out of Jodi's mouth. "He's right upstairs."

"Yeah, I saw him. Old as a rock."

"He exercises."

The person looked surprised. "Thanks for the info."

"I mean, he'd protect me, if he needed to."

The person didn't have an answer to that, so Jodi continued walking. She felt light-headed—her interactions with strangers never went like this. Jodi didn't like being rude.

There was the crunch of gravel behind her. The person was *following* her.

Her heart was knocking against her ribs. At any moment, she could feel an arm wrap around her neck.

She knew her instinct well. When her father would fake-chase her, she'd collapse with a scream and cover her head. He'd get irritated, telling her to stop being a wimp, to run. But she didn't want to. She'd rather curl into herself than fight back.

She was feeling the instinct to drop and scream, but she forced herself to keep walking, her nose slightly up in the air.

There was the sound of faster crunching, and Jodi's heart shot up into her throat. The person passed her, then spun on a heel and planted their feet. Despite their determination to catch her, their eyes weren't on Jodi. Rather, they were stuck to the phone in their hand. "Can you wait one second?" They walked backwards to keep in-step with Jodi's quickened gait.

"Look, I know what this is about, and I'm two seconds from calling the cops."

The person didn't flinch. In fact, they seemed bored, still looking at their phone. "Go ahead."

"Excuse me?"

"Get the cops here. They know me by now."

Jodi's veins felt icy. "Oh, well, that's *interesting*." She didn't know why she said that, nor why she put so much venom into the last word. She wasn't good with comebacks.

"I'd like them here anyway, just in case you put up a fight."

That stopped Jodi in her tracks. "Excuse me? Why would I be fighting anyone? You're the one getting arrested."

The person put away their phone finally, and pinned Jodi with dark, angry eyes that withered her bowels. "Because I need to search your computer."

Jodi blinked. Cold wind swirled around her like an omen. "You're not doing that."

"Yes, I am."

"I have knives. I will use them all."

The person's eyebrows shot up. "At once?"

"No." Jodi glared up at them.

This person studied Jodi for several long moments. Jodi wanted to squirm—she wasn't used to being seen for so many seconds. Finally, the person spoke again. "You need a centenarian bodyguard, but you'd stab me with several knives if I looked in your computer?"

"It's an expensive computer, and your back would be turned. Look, just tell me what you want—I've dealt with people like you before, and I just want a beer."

"I really doubt you've dealt with people like me."

Jodi gave this person wide berth as she edged around to continue her walk, and had to take a few steps on someone's lawn to make her point. She could still feel the eyes on her back as she headed down the sidewalk.

Then, from behind, "Do you watch the news?"

Jodi debated not answering, but she wanted to end this. Obviously, this was a Jehovah's Witness, spreading the good news, and ignoring their cryptic questions wouldn't necessarily stop them from following her. She stopped and turned. "No. I wait for people to tell me the news, against my better judgement, in the street."

Those dark eyes appraised her, unamused. "So you wouldn't have seen the story on Grant Marlowe."

This wasn't what Jodi expected. The name hit her like a brick. "Grant Marlowe...Grant? My client Grant?"

The person's shoulder twitched in a micro shrug, eyes still testing her, gauging her reaction. "He went to a campsite in the mountains to hot tent camp two weeks ago. He was meant to be there for a few days. He hasn't been seen since."

Jodi's mind reeled. The world tilted as she absorbed this unbelievable concept. *Grant? Missing?* "I...I had no idea."

"It was on all the local news sites."

"I really didn't see it. I stay off social media and news sites, generally. If I saw anything, I didn't connect it to my Grant." Jodi stared at the cracked sidewalk, shock and guilt and worry coursing through her. "How much food did he have?"

"This is info you can get online." The person's tone was clipped and no-nonsense, and Jodi felt the sting. "But right now, I'd like your—"

"Why didn't the police contact me?" Jodi wrung her hands. "I'd like to have known. I'm a friend, kind of. And I could have helped."

The person's brows raised in surprise. "I'm sure they didn't even know you existed. I didn't, either, until I found Dad's notebook. He was writing down video ideas and mentioned your name."

Only one word resonated in Jodi's brain. "*Dad?* Grant is your father?"

That micro shrug, accompanied with a sliver of a nod.

"He never mentioned—"

"Nope, he wouldn't."

Jodi bit her lip, then weakly lifted a hand and gestured to the direction she'd been heading in. "Did you want to share a flight of beer? There's a great place down the road, makes a helluva grilled cheese. We can talk—"

"No." The person reached in their pocket, pulled out a wallet, and tugged out a card, which they held out for Jodi between two long fingers. "What I need are the videos."

Jodi blinked. "Which ones?"

"All of them. All the uncut footage from the videos he posted online."

Jodi frowned. "I don't keep the uncut footage."

Anger flashed over their face. "You're kidding me. Why the hell wouldn't you keep it?"

Jodi was about at her limit with this rude person. She abhorred rudeness; never allowing it herself, she resented anyone who used it so freely. "What is your name?"

"Rae."

"Well, Rae, I assume you know your dad pretty well. When he starts up on a story of his, how long does he talk?"

Rae jerked their head. "Depends on when I hang up."

There's a nugget to unpack there. "Well, if you don't, then he can keep going. With one story, he can evaporate a half hour of my afternoon—unpaid, which is a bummer."

Jodi reached up and took the card from Rae's hand. "When alone in the woods, he can go for hours. Unbroken speech, it's amazing. He'll have his camera going into the wee hours of the night, just going on, recording pitch black. 4K footage of nothing but a tent wall. He gets about four hours for every hundred and sixty-four gig card, and he uses up at least five cards each trip. He's bringing me a terabyte of data every few weeks. Since it's not very logical for me to have a computer with thirty extra terabytes of storage to account for a single year of one client's raw footage, yes, I do delete after I've exported the finished videos. Make sense?"

Rae didn't seem abashed, as Jodi wished they'd be. Instead, they waved their hand, as though batting Jodi's defence away like an irksome fly. "Is there anything you kept? Any footage that hasn't seen the internet?"

"No. He was supposed to have given me new footage at the session he'd missed."

Rae's mouth thinned. "How do I know you're not lying?"

"Pardon my asking, but why do you even want the footage?" Jodi hoped there wasn't anyone listening nearby. It was embarrassing having this heated conversation in the street. God forbid anyone was recording—you never knew, these days. "Grant doesn't let me cut much. Typically just long pauses and anytime he falls asleep recording, and even then he sometimes makes me keep a snore or a fart."

Jodi didn't like the look on Rae's face. Partly because she didn't like dealing with anger, but also because she could see the disappointment in their eyes. They'd thought she had something useful. "It would be pretty safe to say that, at this point, I am grasping at a very limited number of straws."

Jodi's anger faded. "If I think of anything, I'll let you know." She indicated with the card and tucked it into her bag. "But is there anything else I can do? Any search party I can join?" The thought of traipsing through wet, cold forest was about as unappealing as a garbage water cocktail, but Jodi pushed the thought aside. The guilt was lapping at her brain; she had plenty of room on her computer. The last session could've been saved, easy. She just liked having a clear hard drive.

Rae shook their head. "The search parties have been reduced significantly. They can't search forever for missing campers, especially when all signs indicate they'd been eaten by a bear."

The blood ran from Jodi's face. "Bear? What? Did they—"

"Give me a call if you find any uncut footage, okay? You look smart. You can figure something out." Rae headed back in the direction of Jodi's house, where she assumed they'd parked their car. She was left alone on the sidewalk, shock still making her heart pound hard.

Chapter 3

Jodi had lost all desire to drink her flight. Instead, after waiting long enough for Rae to have driven off, she went home, grabbed her car, and drove to her mother's.

Her mother opened on the first knock, hands up like a surgeon. "Hi, baby! Sorry, was just washing my hands." She held out her damp hands, tentatively asking for a hug, which Jodi gave. "What's the occasion?"

"Nothing, really."

"So you just wanted to chat, is that it?" Her mother was delighted.

"Pretty much."

"Come on in. The bread will be ready in a few minutes." Her mother retreated inside, hurrying to the kitchen. "Last time I made bread was when your father wanted some, and the store was out because that big semi crashed. Remember?"

Jodi strode down the hallway of her childhood home, running fingers along ancient rips in the wallpaper. "No."

"Oh, well..." Her mother trailed off, then busied herself searching for something in the kitchen. "I'm trying to impress Sonali—you remember Sonali, she babysat you a couple times. Your father didn't like her very much."

"I know Sonali, yeah."

"She's really not all that bad, Jodi. She goes to my Zumba class, and we started talking about bread. She's into sourdough, says it's the best for hearts." Her mother got quiet. "I suppose I should've started making it sooner."

Jodi focused on the flour-covered mixer, sticky with dough. "A loaf of sourdough wasn't going to help Dad's heart, Ma."

Her mother waved a hand, flicking the thought away. "Anyway, she's got these gorgeous, puffy loaves, and I keep making stepping stones. We were going to trade next class." She sighed, then a smile lit her face again, and she shook her head. "I'm still baffled why you didn't hit it off with Evelyn, baby. She's *such* a nice girl."

"We didn't click." Jodi had had this conversation at least five times with her mother over the past few weeks.

"You can't afford to be—"

"I'm not being picky. She didn't feel we clicked, either."

"Well, baby, your father and I didn't click right away. It took time. Back in the day, you never knew after one date, and you never pretended to know. You waited, and all that fake personality we put on at the beginning falls away. You get to really *know* them."

Jodi forced herself to nod.

"In fact." Her mother slipped on the pair of thrice burnt, heavily stained oven mitts that had not left this kitchen for thirty years. "When I first met your father, I couldn't stand him." She nodded sagely, as though this were shocking.

"I getcha, Mum. But I think I'll wait for someone I can stand."

"You can't be picky."

"I can have that single piece of criteria, I think."

"I think your main criteria should be finding someone who can stand *you*." Her mother nodded again, her eyes far away. "I wasn't exactly a catch, back then, you know. Your father was way out of my league."

That familiar sentence bounced in Jodi's brain like a knife in a garbage disposal. "Mum, I was wondering if there's still stuff here that I'd left behind, or anything of Dad's you were going to give away."

Surprise crossed her mother's face. "Yes, there's some stuff. An old bike, some records. Stuff I've not gotten around to giving to the Sally Ann. But you don't have the room, why take them?"

Because I want to sell them. "Just do. Might find something I want to keep."

Her mother bent down and pulled the bread from the oven, sighing when she saw the sunken top. "Again."

"Sorry, Mum. I'll have a piece when it's cool. Stuff's in Dad's office?" She backed into the hallway, then headed towards the room her father had spent ninety percent of his time in.

Her mother called after her, "If you were hoping for any of his old work, I've been putting it in recycling. All spreadsheets and reports, nothing I could make sense of, but you're welcome to root around."

Jodi wanted to laugh at the idea of keeping her father's work documents. "No, that's okay."

Jodi stood at the door of her father's office, gazing at the boxes on the floor. It had been three years since he died. Jodi never could decide whether her mother didn't throw things away because of grief, or because there was always the niggling voice of a dead man in her brain, telling her she was doing something wrong, making fun of her for not understanding the value of his records and spreadsheets.

Jodi knelt and yanked a box of albums towards her, and accidentally knocked over a recycle bin. She was stuffing the papers back into the can when a thought occurred to her.

Oh. Shit.

* * *

Jodi dropped the box of albums off on her bed, then sped back into the living room and flopped into her desk chair. She waited impatiently as her computer booted, then navigated to a place she kept forgetting to empty.

Her recycle bin.

It loaded, and there it was. An entire camping trip's worth of raw footage, unemptied.

Heart pounding, she selected all of them, then hit *restore*.

As they reloaded, she pulled from her bag the business card Rae had given her. All information was scribbled out, save for the name and number. All she had to do was text it.

For a few minutes she tapped absently on the black screen, nervous about texting this stranger and not knowing why. Possibly because Rae had not been the friendliest of people, and she wasn't keen on dealing with more unpleasant conversation. Truth be told, she didn't have a moral obligation to text them at all; she knew what was in these videos. A whole lot of nothing.

Still, that look in Rae's eyes was emblazoned in her mind. That veiled desperation.

So she opened up a new text conversation.

Hey, this is Jodi, your dad's editor. I still have some footage that I hadn't fully deleted. You're welcome to it.

Jodi put her phone down. Then she went online and began the somber search for work. Video Editors and Social Media Managers glutted the market of possible jobs, and she wasn't hopeful, but she needed to try. *And if that fails...there's still Dollarama.*

There was a loud *buzz,* her phone skittering across her desk. She picked it up and saw a new message from that unfamiliar name. *Rae.*

I don't have a computer. I'd like you to go through it with me.

Jodi placed her phone back on the desk and made a face at it, as though Rae could see through the phone. She did not like pushy people. Her history as a textbook pushover made her a target, and she knew it was obvious even to strangers.

Rae must know they had the guilt card to play. Jodi had said she wanted to help. But there was hours and hours of footage to go through. If Rae was anything like Grant, it would take at least twice as long to scrub through, depending on what Rae's plan was for it.

So, she texted back: *As much as I want to help, you would get better results faster if you watched the footage yourself. My days in the near future are going to be taken up with job hunting.*

She typed and retyped several other excuses and offered solutions, but in the end sent simply the two sentences.

Searching on foot for Grant was one thing. But this...this she knew would yield nothing. And she just couldn't handle the thought of spending hours and hours unpacking absolutely nothing with an unfriendly stranger.

She was listlessly clicking on yet another job listing out of her range when her phone buzzed again.

I will pay you what my father did.

She blinked at this message. Then she furiously typed a reply: *You'll pay $30 an hour for me to hit "play" and "pause"?*

Yes.

You realize that in four hours of paying me, you could buy a computer to watch the footage on?

Now I can see why you struggle making rent.

What do you mean by that?

Just take the money.

* * *

"I don't want this person in my house."

Jodi leaned unhappily against the shelves of grass seed, wishing Buckerfield's had benches to sit on. Harper's eyes were crossed and her freshly threaded brows furrowed as she read the back of a mole trap package. "You let them in already."

"That was against my will."

"You didn't say they *forced* their way in. If they did, you need to call the police—"

"No, I allowed it, but reluctantly." Jodi pushed off the shelf and wandered over to a glass case, inside of which were ten yellow chicks. "I wonder if Mr. Doucette would let me get chickens."

"You've not the funds to be asking that, girlie."

Jodi sighed. "At least I'll be getting some blood money from Rae. They'll be at my place at ten tomorrow morning. But how do I even act with this? It feels so wrong. Their dad is missing, and I'm charging by the hour to search his final recorded moments."

Harper didn't seem interested in Jodi's dilemma. "I'm a little worried at the trust you put into people, Jodi. What if this person's a whacko? Your name could, at this very moment, be circulating the sicko network, letting all of them know you're willing to let anyone on Earth use your toilet."

"Tell me something I don't know. But listen, they aren't lying about who they are. I looked up the story." Jodi pulled out her phone and brought up the news article she'd read three times by now. "'*Rae Marlowe, child of Grant Marlowe, provided searchers with a list of items usually taken on Grant's camping trips...*' Look, it's a picture."

Harper took Jodi's phone, a frown on her face. "I don't like their look."

"You can barely see them."

"They give off a suspicious energy."

Jodi wanted to sigh, but refrained. Harper made snap judgements, but they were not always right.

She'd liked Vicki, after all.

Harper's frown deepened as she scrolled. "This doesn't look good, Jodi. Their dad's been missing for two weeks, food only for three days...temperature got in the negatives at night."

"I know."

"His truck was parked in the site, and a lot of his stuff was still set up there, except for some major things. His stove and tent were missing."

"Yep."

"So why does this person think their dad is alive?"

Jodi picked up a bucket of compost starter and pretended to be fascinated so she wouldn't let her annoyance show. Harper was right. But Grant was more than a name in a newspaper article to Jodi. He was someone she knew, and she didn't like her friend diagnosing the situation so offhandedly. "I guess they want to cover all bases. Look under every rock."

"Seems hopeless."

"Harper." Jodi put the bucket down and gave her friend her most patient frown. "If Evan was missing, you'd be searching for months."

Harper went back to looking at the mole traps. "If Evan disappeared into the woods, I'd assume he died within half an hour."

"You wouldn't. You'd have hope."

"He has the confidence of a much more competent man, Jodi." Harper dropped the mole traps into her basket, her eyes melancholy. "Can I tell you something? And can you please please please please not judge me too hard?"

"Sure, man."

"I really wish I could sleep with someone else. Just once."

Jodi blinked. "Because of Evan's sleep apnea?"

"No. Like…" Harper undulated in an exaggerated way with her hips, the basket clunking with the mole traps.

"Please stop that."

"I'm serious. You know what I'd love?" Harper dropped her voice. "I'd love to sleep with someone who knows what they're doing. Just to see if my body's capable of more than *hm, thanks* kinda orgasms, you know?"

"I wish we weren't discussing orgasms in the animal trap aisle." Jodi grabbed a mole trap and studied it, face hot.

"How are your orgasms?"

Jodi thought about it. "Like a MurderMole Mole Trap." At Harper's confused face, Jodi held up the package so the slogan was visible. *"It Gets The Job Done."*

* * *

At ten on the dot, there was a sharp knock on the door. Jodi, who was cleaning up the last of her lychee cans, jumped at the sound.

With a year of Grant being five to ten minutes late to every session—on good days—she'd grown used to leaping into cleaning mode mere minutes before their scheduled time. It was Jodi's mistake for thinking Rae had inherited their dad's late gene. After stuffing the bag of cans into a closet, she hurried to the door.

Rae eyed the doorframe before stepping inside, and Jodi was automatically self-conscious, despite knowing there was nothing wrong with her door frame. Rae unwound a scarf from their neck and balled it up between their hands.

Their eyes then fell to Jodi's feet, which were bare. Their eyes rose to meet hers, questioning.

"You can keep your shoes on, if you'd like." Jodi closed the door. "Your dad kept his on."

Rae toed off their shoes. "So at what point did your conscience get to you?"

Jodi, who was heading into the laundry room where her kettle lived, paused with a confused look back at Rae. "My conscience?"

"About the videos. What made you decide to let me see them?"

"I didn't have any moment. I forgot they were in my recycle bin."

Rae's eyebrow tweaked, in a *yeah, sure* way that immediately irritated Jodi. Still, she stayed pleasant. "Would you like some coffee? Tea?"

Rae had already sat in the chair next to Jodi's, the chair their father usually occupied. "No." They gestured to the computer. "If you don't mind, I'd rather not make this a hang out session. I'm here to look at the footage, not chat and drink tea."

Jodi's pleasant veneer was cracking. "Fair. But I'm going to make myself coffee, if you don't mind."

After making her coffee, Jodi went to the computer and flicked it on, then navigated to the editing program where she'd imported all the footage. She hit the spacebar, and the footage began from the start: a shaking shot of a truck bed, half-packed.

And so, they watched. They watched the unedited footage of Grant packing up, driving, and setting up camp for three solid hours. Every once in a while, Rae would tell her to pause, and they'd write something down. Then, "Go," and Jodi would start up again.

Though her job was limited to the infrequent press of a button—and the occasional zoom or brighten—Jodi was screaming for a break fifteen minutes in. At least when she worked with Grant, she was busy—a cut here, an animation there, a text or transition addition, a PNG of a hat edited onto his head for comedy. Often, they'd use fast-motion or skip over long pauses. But Rae watched every single frame at normal speed, brows furrowed, one socked foot on the chair, leaning against their leg. And for

Jodi, it was more torturously boring than watching Harper's newly seeded lawn grow.

She could very easily go on her phone as Rae watched, but felt it was wrong, considering she was being paid. But as the minutes and hours ticked by, she wondered more and more why Rae didn't just take the footage themselves. There was at least twenty hours to scrub through, and if Rae kept at this pace, they were looking at a six-hundred-dollar fee.

It was when they were starting their fourth hour that an email notification popped up on the bottom of Jodi's computer screen. Unfortunately her hand was not on the mouse, so the notification stayed there for a good two seconds before she could exit it.

New Comment: "People like you shouldn't fucking exist."

Immediately after closing the notification, Jodi hit *play* on the footage. She wasn't sure if Rae had even seen the email, but if they did, Jodi wanted it clear that this wasn't something she wanted to discuss.

Not that Rae seemed the type to pry, or pay much attention to the lives of others. At their first meeting, Rae had the pushy, assuming personality of someone who made anywhere their home, regardless of how others felt about it.

No. Not their home. Rae didn't seem a homey person. No, they were simply the type to see everything as a means to an end. Jodi was a person who held videos that Rae needed. Simple as that. Jodi had gotten a similar vibe from Grant. Jodi was an air fryer, to both parent and child.

It was one of the only characteristics Rae shared with Grant. There were no real visual similarities. Grant was stocky, with a round face, button nose, and bright, if slightly distracted eyes. He had a beard forever a few days past a trim, his trademark rattail down his neck, and always wore a well-used pair of cargo shorts, Hawaiian shirt, and scuffed up hiking boots caked in the dirt of a hundred campsites and trails. His oatmeal complexion featured wide patches of permanent sunburn.

Rae, on the other hand, had none of Grant's rounded roughness. Their features were sharp and angular, with that long, curved nose and taupe skin smooth as glass. Jodi had found her eyes straying to long-fingered, capable hands as Rae fiddled with the pen.

Jodi's phone buzzed. The footage was still rolling, with Rae's eyes fixed on the screen, so Jodi covertly slipped her phone from the table and checked it. It was a text from Harper.

How's it going with the Shit Hawk?

Jodi bit her lip to prevent a smile from breaking out. She had no idea why Harper had landed on that name. She tapped a reply. *I don't even rewatch movies I like.*

We're going on twenty minutes of Grant forgetting the camera was on and filming the inside of his pocket.

I wish you were free. I need you to help me drown these moles.

Sounds like the most exciting thing imaginable at this moment.

I also would like you to take my mind off my mind. I have a Development.

Oh no.

Let me know when the Shit Hawk leaves.

"Shit Hawk?"

Jodi jerked in surprise and her head snapped up to see Rae no longer looking at the screen. Their eyes were on her, and while she couldn't tell what their expression meant—mostly confusion—all she could conclude was that they'd looked at her phone long enough to read Harper's words.

"Why were you looking at my phone?" The words slipped out before Jodi could edit them into something more polite.

"I said *pause* and you didn't hear me. So I turned, and I accidentally looked down and saw—"

"What gives you the right to read my private messages?" Politeness was now far in the distance—Jodi was fighting to not yell.

"Relax. There's nothing in there of interest to me."

"I don't care if you're not interested. You come into my house and assume you can just sit down, and put your foot up on my chair, and then you stick your nosy little eyes into my phone—"

Rae's eyebrows went up. "Stick my—what—"

"We've done enough today. We've spent hours at this now, and I have to get ready to go on a date." The lie was the first thing that came to mind—despite her distress and anger, it was instinctual to give a reason to kick Rae out.

Rae stood and slipped on their shoes. Without another word, Rae left, closing the door sharply behind them.

Jodi sat back in her computer chair, heart thundering. She realized that she was holding her phone in a death grip, and let it drop on her lap. She stared at the ceiling as her heartrate slowly returned to normal, and the guilt began its inevitable uprising in her gut.

She stood, jammed on her runners, and went outside, where she jogged up the stairs and over to Harper's. Right as she was heading down the path to the front door, her friend opened it and stepped outside, wrapped in the thick mint cloak that gave her terrifying majesty. "Oh." Harper's face brightened, though her eyes were shifting as she grabbed Jodi's arm on her frenzied speedwalk towards the car, kicking a filled bag of cans along the way. "Stupid cans—keep meaning to drop them at the depot."

"I was a real ass, Harper—"

"We'll talk in the car."

"Where are we going?"

"I want coffee. Also I'd like you to confirm something for me."

* * *

Jodi hadn't expected to be back at Buckerfield's again so soon, but that's exactly where Harper drove after they'd stopped at the café. They didn't, however, go inside. Instead, they stayed in the car, fogging up the cold windshield, which Harper kept impatiently wiping clear with her cashmere sleeve.

"Why are we staying in the car?" Jodi asked.

"Because we were here yesterday."

"So? Who cares?"

"Jodi, do you remember what I talked about yesterday?"

"Unfortunately." Jodi studied her friend. "This is about...that hypothetical situation you wanted to be in, correct?"

"Yes. Hypothetical, exactly." Harper took a violent sip of her latte. "You get mosquito bites?"

"Yes?"

"It's like that. I can't stop itching it."

Jodi didn't really like this conversation. Even if she wasn't preoccupied with her uncalled-for blowup at Rae—she knew now how nuts she sounded—she didn't want to discuss the potential destruction of her friend's marriage, even if it was hypothetical.

"It happens in many marriages. Seven-year itch."

"I've been married four."

"It's an expression." Jodi put her cup in the holder. "Scratching bites just make them worse, don't you think?"

Harper sighed, looking up at the ceiling of the car. "You're probably right." She scratched her arm absently. Then her head fell back down, and she grabbed Jodi's sleeve. "There he is."

"Who?" Jodi followed her friend's gaze and landed on a tall guy exiting Buckerfield's.

"I asked him where the mole traps were yesterday, remember?" Harper leaned against the steering wheel, a faraway look in her eyes. "You know, I never realized how long it's been since someone flirted with me. God, not since university. It's like I'm fading more and more, every year."

"Your opacity is going down."

Harper shot Jodi a frown.

"Sorry."

"He flirted with me. Said I looked the type to catch a mole on the first try."

Jodi wanted to tell her friend that she might be reading too much into it. But she didn't feel it was the time. Harper wasn't actually considering cheating. She was feeling vulnerable, that's all.

"I think I'm going to do it."

Jodi snapped to attention. "What?"

"I'm going to try and sleep with the Buckerfield's guy."

Damn. "Harper, no—are you sure? I mean—that's not your deal, you've never done anything like this—"

"Yeah, exactly." Harper nodded sharply and opened the door. Before Jodi could say a word, Harper was outside and trudging across the lot, green cloak billowing behind her.

"Goddamn." Jodi struggled to unclip her belt, then exited the car and ran towards a purposefully striding Harper, who had just about reached the Buckerfield's guy as he was unlocking his little Honda Fit.

But then, Harper said nothing. She continued past him, not even slowing down. In fact, the guy didn't even notice her; he noticed Jodi, who did a loud, crunching slow down from her momentary sprint and was now trying to act casual as she passed his car, chest heaving.

Catching up with Harper at the front of the store, Jodi gave her friend a pointed look.

Harper was grinning. "Scared you, didn't I?"

"What the hell? Why did you do that?"

"You were looking all worried. Don't worry—I'm not going to do anything." Harper gazed over Jodi's shoulder. "I just wanted to window shop."

"I'm not in the best mind-state for games, Harper. I just freaked out on a person for accidentally looking at my phone screen." Jodi sat down on the curb. "When am I going to stop being a nutcase."

Harper motioned like she was going to sit, then appeared to think better of it. The curb was damp—Jodi could feel it through her overalls. "I would've freaked out. I hate it when Evan looks at my phone."

"It was an accident."

"Yeah, according to them. But it's never an accident." She shrugged. "This is a good thing. You didn't want to work with them anyway."

Jodi didn't want to explain it to Harper. She didn't want to explain the duty she felt. That she already felt guilty for taking money. That the night before, she had woken from a nightmare that formed a permanent nugget of horror in her stomach. She'd been in the woods and smelled something foul. Running from the smell only made it stronger, and in the back of her mind, she knew the smell was Grant, decaying on the forest floor.

So she just said, "It was easy work." Jodi dragged her hands down her face. "They'd already seen an email I got. It popped up on my computer, so it wasn't their fault. But I was embarrassed. And then, seeing that message from you...I don't know. I feel like I've always got two strikes against me, even if I've just met someone." Jodi snorted. "And then I strike out by being an idiot."

"What was the email?"

"Just...it was a comment."

"What kind of comment?"

"Nothing bad." The lie came easy. "But it was still embarrassing. Don't call them Shit Hawk anymore, okay?"

Harper made a *Scout's Honour* sign, her eyes still focused on the middle distance, where Buckerfield's Guy was starting his car. "I don't even think you should contact this person again, Jodi. I hate to say it, I'm sorry, I know you knew the father, but it was always just blind hope anyway. You can find a less depressing job with a less annoying client."

* * *

Later that night, Jodi lay in her bed, staring at the popcorn ceiling.

She was worried about going to sleep. Her nightmare from the night before was still haunting her, and she was still going over what she'd said to Rae, and Harper's contribution.

She picked up her phone from her chest. No new messages.

With a heavy sigh, she opened the app, and slowly tapped out a message. It took her fifteen minutes to construct the text—it went from a large block of excuses and re-apologies to a simple set of statements.

I acted like a jerk, and I'm so sorry. I'm sensitive to people looking at my phone, it's a me thing, not you. If you want the footage,

I can put it on an external drive. No charge for the session.

She sent the message and dropped the phone back on her chest. She was dreading the reply, and visions of what it could be played through her head. *You're a lunatic. What right do you have to talk to someone that way? My father is missing, you're doing a paid job, and all you care about is that I saw some stupid message on your phone?*

Or they'd never even reply. That seemed a good possibility.

The phone buzzed on Jodi's chest, and she snatched it up.

Doesn't matter. Tomorrow's session is still on. Still going to pay you, stop telling me not to. It's unprofessional.

Jodi blinked. Then she typed furiously. *I made it unprofessional by kicking you out.*

Yes. Exactly. You're making it worse.

Jodi's guilt was fast disappearing. In fact, she felt like yelling at this person again. But she just replied, *Okay,* and left it at that.

And then, from across her bedroom, came a noise that made Jodi nearly hit the ceiling. A soft, raspy, plaintive *pbbbt?*

Jodi's phone hit the carpeted floor as she sat bolt upright, and all she saw was a flash of colour as something left her doorway. Immediately Jodi was out of bed and hurrying out of the room, and it was in her living room where she saw the two shining eyes locked onto hers.

It was a cat. It was fluffy, but dirty, and it was on her couch, ready to run again.

"Hey." Jodi took a tentative step forward, and the cat twitched. "How did you get in?"

Jodi's eyes flicked around, and she spotted the culprit; the window by her workstation was open half a foot. It had been broken into before Jodi moved in, and she couldn't do a thing about the busted lock and hinge except jam it shut with a sawed pool cue. Tonight she'd removed the cue for some air and forgot to replace it.

Jodi knelt and did a few *psspsspss* with fingers outstretched. This was all the cat needed; it hopped off the couch and went up to her hand, sniffing, then dragging its face harshly across Jodi's nails. Jodi pet it for a couple minutes, then grabbed her phone from the room and took a few pictures of the creature. Then she went to the door and opened it. "There you go."

The cat blinked, then walked slowly to the door and lay down on the threshold.

"Great." Jodi nudged the cat with her foot, and it didn't move. She sighed, then looked up and saw something that made her stomach plummet. It was a package, sitting on her welcome mat. Biting her lip hard, she sat down next to the cat and picked up the package. It took her a full minute to open it, and when she did, it only confirmed the dread in her stomach. Another packet of floss. No-name brand.

Jodi threw the package inside, and the cat's head came up. Jodi stroked the cat's ears until her hand was too cold. Then, seeing that the cat had no intention of going back into the chill of the night air, Jodi clumsily scooped the critter off the floor and went back inside.

Chapter 4

Jodi was tearing the top off a bag of cat food when there was a knock on her door. She threw a "Stay there," to the cat, who had curled her way into Jodi's wadded-up robe.

Jodi opened the door. Rae's face was still the same; angular and unsmiling. There was a spark of shock, however, when they spotted the newest addition to Jodi's house over her shoulder. "I didn't know you had a cat."

"I didn't." Jodi stepped back to let Rae inside. "I'm sorry, are you allergic?"

Rae shook their head. "It would suck if I was, considering my job." To Jodi's surprise, Rae knelt and whispered, in an uncharacteristically tender voice, several *c'mere's* to the cat, who—being the suck she was—immediately leapt out of the robe and jammed her face into Rae's outstretched hand. "What's their name?"

"Mini Wheats."

Rae coughed. "I haven't heard that one. I hear a lot, too." Their eyes fell on the bowl in Jodi's hand. "Did you name them after your breakfast?"

"Yes. But this isn't my breakfast, it's hers."

Rae stood. "What brand is it?"

Jodi motioned to the bag, and Rae shook their head. "Should've gotten something a bit better than that. It's barely food."

Jodi placed the bowl a bit roughly onto the ground, and Mini Wheats shot to it. "I am on a budget, thanks. I'm sure she'll be fine with it until she's back with her owner."

"Could've gotten a smaller bag, then."

"What are you, a pet food salesman?"

"I'm a pet groomer."

"Oh." Jodi's face flushed. "Then I guess you know what you're talking about." She crumpled up the top of the food bag and headed for the laundry room. "Why was that information scribbled out on the card?"

"Information is old. Place I work has a different name." Rae was on the floor again, sliding their hand along Mini Wheats' spine. "I'm sure this girl's just happy with any food. I hope the owner isn't a friend of yours, because I'd like to have a talk with them about underfeeding their cat."

"I don't know who the owner is. The cat just came through the window last night." Jodi stuffed the bag into her cupboard.

"She must be a stray, then. Covered in mats, and..." Rae parted some hair and squinted. "Fleas. Infested. Jesus."

Jodi's stomach flipped. "Oh, crap." Immediately her skin was crawling.

Mini Wheats let out a chirrup.

"Poor baby," Rae murmured, and something about the way they said it made Jodi's stomach flip. She ignored it. Rae focused on Jodi. "You need to take care of this."

Jodi resented their tone; like she'd hand-placed the fleas herself. "Okay. You're the groomer. I'll do a few hours of work free. Do something."

Rae pulled Jodi's robe from the couch, gently placed Mini Wheats in the middle, then gathered robe and cat as one and stood. "Let's go."

"Wait, what?"

"We'll go to my work. I'll give her a fleabath and dip her, and then get these mats off. This cat is in serious discomfort."

"Oh, but—"

"Unless you want your house infested with fleas."

"No, I don't want that." Jodi's brain flashed back to Mr. Doucette, asking if she had a cat. She hadn't even remembered that conversation until this moment, and now wondered if he'd seen Mini Wheats wandering around and assumed she was Jodi's. She thought about Mr. Doucette waking up one day to a house jumping with fleas, and her subsequent ejection into the street with a miserable half-eaten Mini Wheats in her arms.

Jodi jammed on her Vans and whipped on her mackinaw, expecting to feel bugs crawling inside. Then she ran to her printer, where she grabbed a stack of still-warm papers. "Should we put these up on the way?"

Rae looked at the stack of fliers that Jodi had made in five minutes that morning with Mini Wheats' picture and Jodi's number. "I'd rather not stop to staple up posters."

"We wouldn't be stapling them because I don't have a stapler." Jodi held up tape and a ball of garden twine she'd found at the back of a drawer. "Tape for things that'll take tape, and string for poles and trees."

Rae seemed in pain at the sight of the string. "Listen. This kind of infestation and matting doesn't happen overnight. You can put those up, but I'd seriously doubt anyone's going to call."

Jodi followed them out of the house and up the cement stairs. Rae was parked in the street—a newer car. Jodi wished she knew cars. At most she could identify the brand.

"Jodi?"

Jodi turned to see Harper out front, getting into her own car on her way to work. Her eyes tracked Rae as they bundled the robe and Mini Wheats into the backseat.

"We're just..." Jodi trailed off. "Getting coffee." She wasn't sure how to explain the situation, especially considering the cat that had not existed yesterday. And she could never be sure if Mr. Doucette was peeking out of his blinds from the upstairs.

Harper nodded slowly, the wheels turning. Then she smiled stiffly at Jodi and got into her car. Jodi didn't know what this meant, but put it out of her mind as she climbed into the passenger seat next to Rae.

Jodi never knew the etiquette with cars. You complimented houses when you first entered, but was it the same with vehicles? She didn't know what to comment on—there wasn't any personalizations. Nothing hanging from the mirror, no dancing hula lady, no eight-ball gearshift. Not even a half-empty Tim Hortons cup in the holder. So Jodi commented on the only thing she knew—the H on the grill. "So, you like driving a Honda?"

"It's a Hyundai."

Jodi looked straight ahead and decided to stay quiet.

Mini Wheats was remarkably calm in the car, letting out only a few anxious meows as they drove. Jodi did her best to calm the cat the only way she knew how—by making fun of it. "You sound like my bathroom door when you meow, Miss Wheats. A soft, fart-like creak. Not a voice for radio, that's for sure."

Mini Wheats chirruped sadly. Rae sighed.

Jodi glanced at them. "Does my talking bug you?"

They shook their head minutely. It felt like a lie, but Jodi tried not to let it bother her. She was well past attempting to hide her annoying traits; she wasn't going to stop just because some moody dog groomer wanted a silent car.

They pulled up to a building. A familiar one. Jodi sat up straight in her seat. "Hey, this place used to be a café."

"Must've been a while back. I've been working here for a couple years."

Jodi had gone here with Vicki, who had loved their bran muffins. Jodi had loved how much Vicki had loved their bran muffins. "They had the most uncomfortable seats. Just planks of wood with really sharp edges. Like we were sitting on a door stop."

"We?"

It was the first question Rae had asked that was about Jodi's life, even obliquely. It was also one of the only questions Jodi did not want to answer. "Yeah. Me and friends."

"That girl next door?"

"Yeah, sure."

"She didn't seem too happy to see you going this morning."

They got out of the car. Rae reached into the backseat and managed to pull out a squirmy Mini Wheats, still wrapped in Jodi's bathrobe. The bathrobe she spent so many nights getting drunk in. Jodi tried not to think about it. "I don't know what she was thinking. She has very impulsive impressions. I never know what she'll assume until she tells me."

"Is she the one who called me Shit Hawk?"

Jodi winced, both at the memory of her freakout and the name. "Yes."

Rae didn't elaborate, thankfully. They just headed for the door, on the front of which was the stencil that Jodi was just now reading. *Noah's Bark Grooming.*

"Does this place only take animals in pairs?"

Rae let out a long exhale through the nose. "Do you know how many times I've heard that joke?"

"No, tell me."

They paused, their hand on the door. "I don't know exactly, but—"

"Then why would I know?" Jodi reached out and pulled the door open for them. "After you." She was embarrassed enough seeing Rae holding her fifteen-year-old tattered robe whose sleeves she'd dipped too many times into boiling macaroni water. She didn't need her jokes to be sighed at.

The place was big and clean and loud, with forest green walls and a big oak desk next to the waist-high door leading to the grooming area. Barking pierced Jodi's ears, along with the whine of clippers and chatter of people. A girl with a high, dark brown ponytail passed by the doorway with a howling husky on a leash held in one hand, and a small crate in the other. The girl's eyes widened at the sight of Rae. "My Treasure! What are you doing back? I thought you were off until..." She trailed off. Jodi hung back awkwardly, the words *My Treasure* pinging around in her head.

"It's an emergency groom." Rae held up the bundle of cat and robe. "You guys don't have to do a thing—this is my own time."

The girl sighed good-naturedly. The husky jumped at the half-door. "No, not yet, Sadie—she's being a real turd today. Knocked this crate and a pair of clippers off the counter. Cracked the crate, and now the clippers rattle like hell. Probably can fix the clippers, but I'm throwing the crate out, the door doesn't shut properly." She lifted the doomed crate over the door and tucked it behind the desk, then gave Rae a look of concern. "Has there been any update on your dad?"

"No update. But I'm still optimistic." Rae's answer was assured. "He's out there. But in the meantime, this little one is covered in fleas."

"Oof. Go right ahead." The girl shot Rae a final smile and pulled the serenading Sadie away.

Rae pushed the half-door open, holding it ajar with their knee for Jodi.

"Are you sure?" Jodi gestured behind her to the seats in the waiting area. "I can just—"

"It'll take me a while. You can help."

Jodi wasn't used to being in...

What was the word?

Places.

For the past two years, Jodi had nestled comfortably into a life of working remotely and never venturing farther than fifty metres from her bed. Her social life ended with her neighbour's house. The most noise she endured was the treadmill of Mr. Doucette a floor above, and the occasional motorcycle that would set her heart pounding at 3AM. Her skin was very used to the specific tactile surfaces and temperature of her basement suite, her nose was blind to any smell that wasn't her own. She ordered groceries off her phone and had gotten very good at trimming her bangs over the bathroom sink.

Every sense was overloaded in this place. The sound of dogs, clippers, and dryers pummeled her ears. The smell of wet fur and shampoo coated her nostrils. It was hot and humid, and water droplets misted her face from a dog shaking his coat dry in a nearby tub. Not to mention, she was overwhelmed by the sheer amount of *life* in this room. Animals and people alike shot her looks of surprise and curiosity as she passed.

"Are you sure it's all right for me to be here?" Jodi hissed to Rae, who had stopped by a tub and deposited Mini Wheats into it.

Rae snapped on some blue gloves. "Yeah, I asked the owner."

"When?"

Rae was busy clipping a leash around Mini Wheats' neck and under her leg and didn't answer. It took Jodi way too many seconds to finally understand what they weren't saying. Rae wasn't employed here—they owned the place.

Jodi leaned forward over the tub, trying to look into Rae's face. "Are you saying *you* called this place Noah's Bark?"

Rae's ears were red, and with delight Jodi realized they were embarrassed. *Good. Even the playing field a bit.*

Jodi watched as Rae set up the bathing system, fiddling with little knobs and levers until foamy water spat from the hose, which they directed at a now miserable Mini Wheats, who was using every possible opportunity to clamber out of the metal tub. Rae never lost patience, simply unplucking the cat from their shirt and arms and placing her back into the bathtub to resume the scrubbing.

As the bathing continued, Rae started explaining the steps of the bathing process. Jodi was surprised, then realized she was gripping the side of the tub so hard that Rae probably thought she was anxious watching Mini Wheats be tortured. Probably thought she was seconds away from shutting down the procedure altogether.

She *was* anxious. She didn't like visiting someone else's work. She didn't like being surrounded by noise. But this was for Mini Wheats, and Rae was doing her a massive favour.

To distract herself, she focused on her immediate surroundings outside the tub, and landed on a collection of Polaroid photos stuck to the wall with blue tack. There were a lot of dejected-looking dogs, and some of dejected-looking people. Above the photos were several pieces of paper forming a sign, printed on a printer running low on toner. *"We Did Do That Here."*

"'We did do that here,'" Jodi read aloud. "What does that mean?"

Rae spared a glance at the board before going back to a struggling Mini Wheats. "If you stay here long enough, you'll start hearing one sentence a lot."

"What?"

"'We don't do that here.'" Rae pulled Mini Wheats, once more, from the edge of the tub, then leaned down and said, in a kind, firm tone, "We don't do that here, Mini Wheats." Rae gestured with a wet hand to the board. "Those capture particular moments where pets or people did, in fact, do that here. Bit someone, or pooped in the bath, or forgot to contact the blade sharpener for the third time in a row."

The ponytailed girl passing by threw Rae an indignant look. "I only did it twice."

"One time pooping in the bath is more than enough."

The girl whacked Rae with the towel she was holding.

Rae faced Jodi, and confusion crossed their face. "I'm kidding. She didn't poop in the bath, not even once."

Jodi realized her face was betraying her thoughts. "No, I wasn't—I'm just thinking."

"It's not that deep. It's just a workplace thing."

"I know. It looks fun."

"That face makes it seem like I said we execute every seventh client."

Jodi forced a smile, and Rae didn't push the subject. They just shook their head in a *well, that was weird* motion and continued bathing Mini Wheats. "How was your date?"

"My what?" Jodi's brain was frazzled, but she was sure she'd remember going on her second date in two years.

"You said yesterday you needed to get ready for a date."

"Oh." That was right. Her reason for kicking Rae out. "It fell through."

"Oh. Sorry."

"Yes, it's a real bummer." Jodi felt like a tool, so she changed the subject. "Why are you shampooing a second time?"

"Cats have very oily coats. They usually go through a few shampoos. This one I'm using is a flea and tick shampoo." They scrubbed Mini Wheats' lower back. "Fleas love this area, so you pay special attention there."

"Why is she bleeding?" Jodi watched the reddish water swirl down the drain.

"She's not. Flea dirt is reddish brown. She's been infested for a while, all the crap is in her fur."

Jodi nodded. "I can't let her back outside, can I?"

Rae gave a half shrug that said *no*.

"My landlord doesn't allow cats. And even if he did, I couldn't afford it."

"You can hand her over to the SPCA."

Jodi didn't love the sound of that, either. "When I tried to let her outside, I got a very bad omen."

Rae squirted some blue shampoo onto their hand and scrubbed it into Mini Wheats' face. "A bad omen. Like a black cat?"

"No. It was a package of dental floss. But for me, it represents bad things. And when I sat down, Mini Wheats comforted me. I feel like something was telling me to take responsibility for her." Jodi reached down and stroked the cat's wet, blueish forehead.

Rae continued spraying the cat down without saying anything. Then, "You shouldn't take her because of a bad omen. Not if you can't afford to keep her."

"I know that. But what are the chances of her actually finding a home otherwise? I'd never get it out of my head."

"There's a danger in being too kind, Jodi."

Her name coming from Rae's mouth did something funny in her stomach. But she also heard the rest of what they'd said. "Who said I was anywhere *near* being too kind?"

"My father wrote it in his notes. *Jodi's a sweet girl. A little too sweet. Can't be too hard on her, I think she'd crumple up like wet tissue.*"

"Your dad doesn't know me at all."

Rae shut off the bathing system. "Don't take it personally. Like your neighbour, he tends to stick with initial judgements. He still thinks I'm allergic to edamame because I refused to eat it after the fortieth time he made it in one month."

Jodi didn't answer that. She was deep inside her head. The floss was wrapping around her brain and cinching tight.

Rae seemed to sense her daze and dropped the subject. They were mixing something in a bottle, and had continued their little murmured lecture. "This is dip. It's a special flea solution that you leave on the coat. I try not to touch it too much because it's a pesticide—the pets can handle it because they only touch it once, but I'm exposed to it every day..."

"You know I hate this fucking floss. Jesus Christ, what do I have to do? Do I have to scream it at you? Is that what you want?"

Jodi was jolted out of the memory by a wet bundle being placed in her arms. "Take your cat and rub her with the towel. We're going to dry her with Mr. Smith over there and she's going to hate every moment."

"Is Mr. Smith what's making that loud noise?"

"Yes. Our blow dryer. We'll put a hood on her."

"Why Mr. Sm—"

"Client a while back. Blows hot air." Rae didn't seem to notice how Jodi had broken out into a sweat, nor how she was blinking quite a bit more than usual. And of course, they didn't see the toonies that had once more plopped into her stomach, weighing her down to the shiny, hair-covered linoleum they were walking across.

They passed by the girl with the long ponytail, who was brushing out the wailing husky from earlier. The girl threw a tired look at Rae. "I am, once more, deaf in both ears."

"She didn't sing as much this time. I remember a few seconds of silence."

"That was when she puked." The girl's cheerful eyes slid to Jodi. "New blood?"

"No, she's just tagging along."

The two of them continued to the table with the dryer. Jodi's brain was still tied up; she needed to unravel it or there'd be more days of wall-staring. She couldn't have any more of those. *Besides, my wallowing robe is full of fleas.*

So she forced herself to speak. "What's her name?"

"Sadie."

"No, the girl."

"Oh, sorry. That's Alpine."

Rae did what he could with Mini Wheats, brushing out the dead fleas and shed hair and shaving off the mats that had tightened to her skin. At the end she looked like a dishevelled, skinny, half-plucked chicken, but she gave a lick to Rae's hand in reluctant thanks as they sprayed her with pet cologne.

"I'll wash the robe in our machine." Rae clipped a spare collar and leash onto the cat's neck. "Just in case."

"Thanks." Jodi wondered if she'd ever get her robe back. At the moment she didn't care; she just wanted out of the sensory nightmare of this room. The noise she could've handled on its own, but the feeling of watchful eyes was pushing her to a panic.

"Rae!" Alpine hurried towards the two of them. In her hands was a box, which she held up high. "We have a ton of stuff left from the party. These cupcakes are just going to get all sad in the fridge; you need to take them home."

"Thanks."

Alpine's eyes slid to Jodi's. And it could've been her own current state of near panic, but Jodi saw a flash of suspicion in those eyes. And no, she knew it wasn't possible—it was possible, absolutely it was possible—that two people in a month would recognize her...

A blind date set up by her mother was one thing. This was another. This was worse. Jodi was being recognized by someone connected, however obliquely, to a client.

Jodi counted on Grant, despite his very regular posting of videos online, to be internet unaware. His extent of online knowledge began and ended with the bushcrafting and hot tenting community, so she'd felt safe. Even after a year and a half Grant had zero knowledge of Jodi's past, and she'd assumed it'd stay that way.

* * *

They left the building and stepped into the blissful sound of the distant highway. Jodi took a breath, though the bleakness that had entered her brain remained. She knew it would. It never went away easily.

Mini Wheats squirmed in her arms. She focused on that. On the little life she was now, apparently, responsible for.

She glanced at Rae, who was unlocking the car. "Thank you. I don't know what I'd have done about the fleas if you weren't here."

"You'd have taken her to a groomer."

"No." Jodi pondered. "I would've searched online for a home remedy. Bathed her in pickle juice or something."

Rae's face twisted. "You'd have pickled a cat?" They opened the back door for Jodi to deposit Mini Wheats inside.

"If it worked, yeah." Jodi unloaded the cat onto the seat. "I feel like that's a thing. It cleans Tupperware."

"It doesn't."

"It does."

"If it does, it's because of the vinegar. Why wouldn't you just use vinegar?"

80

"Because when I don't have the energy or self-respect to make dinner, I don't cram handfuls of vinegar in my mouth."

Rae and she got into the car. "I can see now," Rae chucked the box of cupcakes in Jodi's lap, "why you got the cat food you did."

Jodi didn't appreciate that. "So are you and Alpine a thing?" The question came from her own annoyance, wanting Rae to feel embarrassed again.

But Rae merely looked surprised as they started the car. "Alpine is an employee."

"She likes you. I can tell."

"How?"

"I have two perfectly functioning eyes, that's how. Making sure you got cupcakes. Calling you My Treasure."

"*My Treasure* is because of a client. She had this absolutely demonic male Chow—heavily featured on the board—who she'd only call *My Treasure*. She'd say it a lot. *My Treasure, please don't snap. My Treasure, you're not going to make friends that way. My Treasure, please let go of their arm, that's a Treasure.*" Rae slapped their thigh. "I've got a couple good scars from *My Treasure.*"

"There?"

"Went right through my jeans."

"It's because you didn't call him *My Treasure.*"

"No, I did. I'm pretty sure it's why he did it."

Jodi laughed, and Rae shot her a look. Not of surprise, or annoyance. It was just a look, and Jodi couldn't decipher what it was. Then her stomach growled, and Jodi realized that while she told Harper they were going to grab coffee, she in reality hadn't eaten a thing today. So she tapped the box in her lap. "Do you want a cupcake?"

Rae's brows went down in confusion at the abrupt question. "No."

"Are you sure?"

"It sounds like *you* want a cupcake."

Jodi shook her head hard, cursing how obvious her ploy was. "Nope. Not at all. Unless you were—"

"Just take a cupcake." A gloomy meow came from the backseat, and Rae reached forward and switched on the heater. "I'm hoping you're still available to help me go through videos today."

Jodi had forgotten, but luckily didn't have any other client work. "Of course. I'll go for as long as you want." Jodi studied the slightly squished frosting on the cupcake she was eating. "Do you...I mean...do you think they're close to finding your dad?"

"I think they'll either find him, or he'll wander out of the woods, unaware of the time that's passed."

It certainly seemed like something Grant would do. "I hope so."

"He will." Rae was nodding hard. "He absolutely will." Their tone left no room for discussion.

* * *

Jodi couldn't sleep that night.

Partly, it was because of Mini Wheats.

After her busy, miserable afternoon, the cat had slept the entire time Rae had been at Jodi's. For five hours, all the way until seven. Then Rae had left, and the door jolted Mini Wheats out of her slumber, at which point she began yowling and winding around Jodi's legs, wanting her dinner. Jodi had worked as quickly as possible, well aware that the sounds this cat was making would put Mr. Doucette's treadmill to shame. It was as though the hair mats had restricted Mini Wheats' lungs from expanding, and their removal had unleashed her entire vocal strength.

Jodi watched Mini Wheats eat. "What am I going to do with you."

She wondered this even harder after turning the light out at bedtime; this was, apparently, Mini Wheats' time to show off her physical prowess. Nothing was off limits—not the shelves, nor the toilet, nor the counters, nor Jodi's bed. Around and around the suite Mini Wheats shot, and when Jodi closed her bedroom door, the cat reprised her dinnertime song until Jodi flung the door open again.

Listening to the rapid thumping of Mini Wheats' paws on the floor, Jodi stared at the ceiling. Even without the cat long-jumping from the desk to the couch, Jodi wouldn't have been able to sleep. Her mind was occupied with thoughts of Grant.

Earlier, she had asked Rae what they were looking for in the videos. "Maybe I can help spot something."

Rae had shrugged, eyes fixed on the screen. "Anything. Any hint of what mood he was in. Any ideas he might've been considering."

"Like what?"

"Like, for example, his desire to ignore his campsite altogether and go deeper into the woods instead." Rae had reached out and tapped the screen. "He's said about six times now that he hates this campsite. *Too phony.* He hates having the table there, and the fire pit."

Jodi knew this. It wasn't the first time Grant had talked ill of the campsites. He disliked anything that made it feel less "legit," including the toilets and the proximity to a phone signal. But she also remembered asking him if he'd ever venture outside the campgrounds, and he'd sighed and said, "No. I'm not at that level yet." She wasn't sure by which measurement he used to classify levels of hottentsmanship, but she hadn't pushed the issue. She hated the thought of him getting lost in the woods.

And he is lost in the woods.

Jodi flipped over in her bed and tucked her duvet closer around her. The air blowing through her cracked window was cold.

She imagined being outside. Having no food, no dry hardwood to light a fire. And once more, she wondered how Rae could possibly think their father was alive.

Jodi had gone online. Searched up news articles, Facebook groups. There was hope, but it had dwindled. The search parties had lessened. People often went missing in the Pacific Northwest woods. The rainforest was like a creature in its own right, ready at any moment to bite and swallow.

The thought of Grant dying alone in the woods horrified her. The thought of being in the woods horrified her, even without the dying part. But she knew her horror couldn't come close to what Rae must be feeling.

She tried it. She tried imagining her own father, lost in the woods. And into her pillow she stifled a giggle.

Her father was the type to say he was an outdoorsman. He would say he was any type of man. But to Jodi, he was simply the type of man to go to his office job, tell people what they were doing wrong, then come home and continue the practice. He was a man who did a very good job of being present in her life; she just hadn't liked it very much. When he'd had his first heart attack, she'd managed to show concern. When he'd died after the second a year later, she'd managed to mourn. But it didn't come easy.

She pressed her face hard into the pillow. *No more thinking about that.* Her mind slipped tentatively towards its other, deeper groove. *Not that, either.*

Then, as if to bother her, it slipped into a new groove. One labeled *Rae.*

She frowned at the furniture blued by moonlight. Why was she still thinking about Rae? They certainly didn't give her a thought any moment they didn't need to.

Still, she couldn't help but wonder what a person *did* when their father was missing. The day would be busy with search efforts, but what about at night? What about right now? Were they awake, feeling the biting wind come through the window?

Did they eat? Did they take any moment to cook, or did they just shovel in four cupcakes and call it a night? Jodi couldn't cook when she was stressed. She was, therefore, a very unpracticed cook.

Jodi's bowels nearly vacated when her phone rang on her dresser, lighting up the dark room. She fumbled with the phone, squinting at the screen, and with relief saw that it was Harper. She answered. "What?"

"Jodi, there's a cat in your suite."

Jodi sighed, throwing an arm over her eyes. "I know. Wait, how did *you* know?"

"I can see a window from my living room. There's a very distinctive shape walking around—when did you get a cat?"

"She wandered into my house yesterday—"

"You can't afford a cat, can you?"

"It's an unexpected expense." Jodi got up and peeked out her bedroom door. "She's running around the place like...like she runs the place."

"Jodi, you invite trouble, you know that?"

Jodi knew Harper was joking around. But the joke did not make her laugh.

"You know what I actually thought happened?"

"What?" Jodi's tone was flat as she climbed back into bed, suddenly tired.

"I thought Shit Hawk had a cat that couldn't be left alone for a night."

"Left alone? What—no, Rae isn't still here!" Jodi was sputtering and holding onto her pillow for dear life. "I just met them! And Lord, are they ever not my type."

"They don't have to be, do they?" Harper heavy-sighed into the phone. "I was thinking about Buckerfield's Guy this morning. Buck. Do you think he's secretly a poet?"

"I think he could be outwardly a poet. You wouldn't know either way because you've never had a non-mole-trap conversation."

"I bet he'd know not to touch the traps with his bare hands."

"Probably. He sells them. Since when have you liked poets?"

"I don't know. But I feel like everyone should date a poet at some point."

Jodi frowned. "Are you drunk?"

"Maybe a little. You haven't come over in days. I've got no one to tell me to stop." There was the sound of a can crinkling as she drank. Harper got personal when she was drunk. "Don't get with Shit Hawk, Jodi."

"I wasn't planning on it."

"Your meet cute is their dad being eaten by a bear. Not the best. They'll always associate you with that."

"We don't know Grant's dead."

"He is, Jodi. I'm sorry, but he is." Harper burped. "You shouldn't give this person false hope, you know? You have a lot of power over other people's feelings."

"You assume a lot."

"I'm a realist."

"I think you should go to bed."

"Have you paid your rent yet? You should be concentrating on that—get the money from this person and move on. Also keep in mind that if your landlord finds you with a cat, he'll kick you out and I won't have anyone to talk to anymore."

"Goodnight, Harper."

"You need to be here, to tell me to stop. I tell you to stop, you tell me to stop, that's the deal." She was slurring now.

"I don't need you to tell me to stop anything."

"You did. You do. You're not..." She sighed. "You're not a relationship-person."

Jodi brought the phone down and pressed *end*. Harper would probably keep talking, unaware the line was dead. Likely wouldn't remember this in the morning.

Again, Jodi got out of bed, then went into the living room. It took her a minute to find Mini Wheats, whose head was stuffed up a lampshade, sniffing the bulb. Jodi pulled her out and sat down on the couch, stroking the cat's bony, patchy spine. "Did you have owners once, Mini Wheats?" Jodi whispered. "Do you miss them? Even if they treated you badly?"

Mini Wheats chirruped and slammed her face into Jodi's hand.

Chapter 5

Jodi's phone brought her out of a doze, and Mini Wheats dug claws into her leg as she shot off the couch. Bleary-eyed and with a pounding headache, Jodi sat herself straight and grabbed her phone. *Rae.*

Her heart thumped strangely; she ignored it and answered. "Hello."

"Did you just wake up?"

Jodi quickly looked back at her phone, and saw the time was eleven thirty. "No, I've been up for hours." After launching off the couch, she went to her laundry room and switched on the kettle.

"I was talking with the search people, and long story short they're going to reduce the search to almost nothing." Rae didn't sound bothered. "They can only focus on one person for so long, makes sense. Don't blame them. Need their resources."

Jodi stared at the coffee grounds in her filter, at a loss for what to say. "I'm...I'm sorry—"

"I won't be able to do any footage today, or tomorrow. Maybe the next day."

She pulled Mini Wheats' food bag to her and fished inside for the scoop. "That's...fine. We hadn't planned any—"

"How's the cat? Did she eat?"

Jodi was fast discovering something about Rae. They were very good at masking their emotions...except for the fact that they wouldn't stop talking. "Yes. Did *you* eat?"

There was a pause. "What?"

"Did you eat? I don't eat when I'm stressed." Mini Wheats was screaming as Jodi rattled some food onto a plate.

"I'm not stressed. And yes, I ate. A lot. Preparing myself to potentially eat nothing this evening. Or tomorrow."

Jodi paused on her way to putting the plate on the floor. Mini Wheats let out a concerned *brrp*. "Why wouldn't you eat?"

"See, this is my thinking. People know my dad set up camp at the site—there were witnesses that remember him doing it. If he got lost in the woods on a hike, why was his tent and stove gone? They just found his other stuff. Wood, chair, things like that."

"They think it's because he didn't want the expensive things stolen." Jodi placed the plate on the floor, and Mini Wheats attacked.

"I don't think that's the reason at all. We know from the videos that he leaves everything behind when he hikes. So what's different now? It must not have been a hike—more like he moved camp. But then, why leave some stuff behind?"

"Hard to carry."

"He left his wood. Why? He needs it to light the stove. Why take the stove and not the wood?"

"He could have taken some of it—"

"See, I don't think he went anywhere on purpose." Rae was talking fast again. "I think he left because he had to, for some reason. On short notice."

Jodi watched Mini Wheats lick the plate. "Something short notice enough for him to take down his tent?"

"I don't know. But something is weird. So I'm going to test it."

"What? How?"

"Tonight, I'm going camping in the same site he was in."

"What?"

"I called, and the person there said no one's been in Dad's site since."

Jodi looked out the window, outside of which a frigid wind rustled leaves off the cherry tree in the yard. "You can't camp now. It's freezing cold."

"Not just camp. Hot tent camp. I've watched enough of my dad's videos to know how."

Jodi sat down heavily on the couch. "You don't have the equipment."

"Yes, I do. I can get into my dad's place. He has more equipment—another tent and stove. It'll work."

"We're in the beginning of a cold snap."

"I'm doing it anyway. There's something weird that made him leave that site, I know it. It's not something as simple as him forgetting his bear spray."

Jodi couldn't help but feel a spike of dread. She didn't believe in ghosts, or curses—but there was something distinctly foolhardy about recreating a trip on which an experienced camper disappeared.

It was doomed to fail, either way. She knew Rae would find nothing, just as she knew they'd find nothing in the videos.

Uneasy, she watched Mini Wheats devour the shitty food.

* * *

Jodi left her place and walked over the cold, crispy grass to knock on Harper's door. It was opened by Evan, holding a phone in one hand and a pickleball paddle in the other. "Oh! Hi..." He smiled blankly at her.

"Jodi."

Evan jerked his head, as though saying *I knew that.* "Harper's still in bed. Not feeling great, might have a flu or something."

Jodi could tell by the sincerity in Evan's concern that he had no clue his wife was drinking into the wee hours of the morning. "I brought over a mug of strong coffee." She held up the mug. "Figured it'd make her feel better."

"Oh...how did you know she was sick?"

Oops. "She texted me."

93

Evan glanced down at the phone in his hand. "I have her phone. She left it downstairs."

Jodi blinked hard. "I am...clearly just saying things to make conversation, Evan. I brought over the coffee because I'm dumb and forgot it was in my hand."

Evan seemed to absorb this excuse. "You can go up, but I don't—"

"Thanks." Jodi edged past him and, after kicking off her shoes, ran up the stairs. After rapping lightly on the bedroom door, she opened it a crack. "Harper? Do you have a touch of death poisoning?"

The pile of blankets rustled. "I fucking hate myself." Harper's voice was two cracks from a death rattle.

Sympathetic—and grateful she wasn't in the same state—Jodi walked over and sat on the side of the bed. "How much did you drink?"

Harper did a soft little retch, almost polite. Jodi moved a couple inches away. "I drank five Colts. Did you know that they're stronger here? US has it at five percent, we've got eight. Didn't know that."

"Of course they're strong. We get loud after one." Jodi set the coffee on the ground.

"Should have the info on the can."

"I would bet rent money that it does."

Harper groaned again. Then a bloodshot eye snapped open, looking at Jodi down the length of the duvet. "You didn't tell Evan, did you?"

"No. He thinks you've got the flu."

"Good." The eye closed. "He'll avoid the room then. Might even break out the air mattress tonight, if I'm lucky. If he knew I was just hungover he'd prance in here, loud as a damn—" She paused. Then she slid out of bed with a hearty thump to the carpet and ran unsteadily to the ensuite bathroom. Jodi winced at the sound of vomit hitting the toilet bowl.

After a few minutes, the toilet flushed and Harper reemerged, pale as milk. "I feel better."

Jodi nodded, wondering if she'd ever seen her friend look worse. "You look great."

"I know." Harper re-entered the bed, then shot another furrowed-brow look to Jodi. "Did you call me last night?"

"No. You called me."

"Right. The cat! You have a cat?"

Jodi shushed her friend. "I currently am housing a cat. I don't know what I'm doing with it."

"And this is *not* Shit Hawk's cat? This is just...some cat?"

"I think Mr. Doucette saw her wandering around before. Asked if she was mine the other day."

"So now he's going to think you're lying."

"No, because you'll have my back. Also, I took a photo of her when she came in, look." Jodi pulled out her phone and showed Harper the picture she took of a ragged-looking Mini Wheats. "She came when I was feeling really rotten. I don't know…I feel like she's important, somehow. Like a cute little harbinger."

"She looks halfway through a spin cycle."

"I know." Jodi flicked through more photos and realized that she'd already taken at least twenty. Ten were of Mini Wheats with her head up the lampshade—it was her favourite spot, aside from Jodi's lap. "Rae took her to their work and cleaned her up. They own a grooming salon."

Harper nodded slowly, like it caused pain at any other speed. "Uh…huh. So you *do* like this person."

"What?" Jodi lowered her phone, on which was a photo of Mini Wheats visiting Jodi in the bathroom. "I just know they own a pet salon. It's a fact."

"Okay. And what facts do they know about you?"

Jodi rubbed her thumb across a dirty spot on her phone screen. "None."

"Not the greatest way to start a relationship."

"I don't need to tell everyone I know, and certainly not Rae. We'll be back to strangers next week—they're a client. That's all."

"A client who helps you care for a cat?"

"She had fleas. Strangely, a client doesn't want to do business in a house infested with fleas."

Harper made a face. "You're not spreading fleas into this house, are you?"

"Yeah, Evan's been eaten alive. Sorry."

Harper studied Jodi, fingers to her dewy temple. "I'm proud of you, you know."

Jodi blinked a few times. "Because I rescued a cat?"

"Because you're managing. You never broke down, not even after everything." Harper tilted her head. "It's pretty amazing."

Jodi swallowed, thinking about her robe. "Yeah, well...I'm good at hiding it."

"You've also never had a rebound. I always needed a rebound post breakup, yet you've just been...alone." Harper reached out and, with clammy fingers, gripped Jodi's hand. "I just hope you're not leaping at any chance, you know. After Evelyn—"

Jodi pulled her hand away. "I'm not *leaping* at anything, Harper. Why are you still pushing this?"

"This person isn't your type. They're intense and complicated, and I just think you might see something that isn't there, that's all. I'm saying this as your friend."

Jodi nodded, not knowing what to say.

"Evelyn," Harper continued, sticking up a finger and wagging it affirmatively, "now she was your type."

"You didn't even meet her."

"Just by how you described her, I can tell. I think that's where you should focus your energy, personally."

"What, on a person who judges me on sight?"

"No. Someone uncomplicated." Harper's eyes landed on her side table. Immediately, her posture stiffened. "Where's my phone?"

"I think Evan—"

"Fuck!" Again, Harper slid out of bed and fell to the floor, but instead of going for the bathroom, she charged for the hallway. Jodi followed, taking the now cold cup of coffee with her.

For someone hungover, Harper sure could move fast. She was already arguing with Evan in the kitchen when Jodi stepped off the last stair.

"I told you not to touch my phone," Harper was saying, holding it up. "I need it to be where I left it. I can't be searching for wherever you happened to put it down."

Evan was spreading jam on some toast, looking uncomfortable. "Don't breathe on me, okay? I don't want to be sick for the tournament next week."

"Did you hear me?"

"Yes, I heard you. Why are you out of bed? I thought you were sick?"

Harper turned on her heel, face stormy. "I am. That's why I need my phone." She brushed past Jodi and went upstairs. Jodi considered following her, but decided against it and slid on her shoes. "Better get back."

Evan didn't seem to be listening; he was chuckling under his breath. "She's always mad at me these days." He shook his head and took a big bite of toast. "What can you do."

Jodi glanced out the window to the backyard, at the hilly dirt. "Kill those moles, and she'll be happy."

Evan chuckled again. "Eh, those moles. Every day, I hear about those moles. She's obsessed."

"She'll be happy when they're gone."

"They'll leave over the winter."

"No, they won't. They'll come back in the spring. Trust me, she's looked it up."

He seemed to consider this, but then took an even bigger bite of the toast. "I'm sure it'll be fine."

Jodi left the house, clutching her mug, then sat down on the chair next to the door to tie her shoes. Her fingers weren't working too well; she kept overdoing the loops. The conversation with Harper was running through her head, tightening around her brain.

It was surprising, the dislike Harper had for Rae. But then, Jodi wondered if it was dislike at all. Her friend seemed more focused on Jodi's state of mind. Concerned that Jodi wouldn't be able to handle someone complicated. Again.

Which was fine. Jodi could understand that concern. But with her mother's advice to settle and her friend's advice to find someone uncomplicated, Jodi wondered if there was anyone on Earth she could be with. According to Drunk Harper, Jodi wasn't a relationship person, and time certainly wasn't on her side.

That concept was a revelation two years ago. She'd just turned thirty and during one of her robe nights had made the mistake of looking in a mirror. The mascara rubbed into her eye-circles and the liquor's pallor made her look ten years older. Worse, it made her look broken.

She *was* broken. It would take time to heal, and in the meantime, she'd only be getting older.

After finally managing to get the shoes tied, Jodi sat up with a groan, pressing her aching back with a hand. That was when she spotted the five Colt 45 cans placed just outside the front door. There was that giant, full bag of empty cans a few feet away, apparently too far (and perhaps too loud) for Drunk Harper to navigate at three in the morning. However, if Evan exited the house, he'd see the cans immediately.

With a sigh, Jodi stood, picked up the cans, and slid them into the bag. Then, after a moment of thought and a glance back at the door, Jodi picked up the bag and took it to her car.

* * *

After returning the cans and emptying her chequing account—which was luckily garnished with a GST cheque coming in clutch—Jodi cleared the amount for rent, with the addition of a couple of coin rolls. The bank cashier had seemed happy for Jodi, who had been unable to keep a celebratory fist-pump at bay. However, Jodi had also thought she'd seen the tiniest spark of recognition in the woman's eye. It was likely pure paranoia brought on by the conversation with Harper, but it had happened before. Jodi wished she had the money to get beauty treatments; a few fillers would make her face too juicy to be recognized.

Harper's words floated through Jodi's brain. *What facts do they know about you?*

It's possible Rae would find out somehow, considering Jodi's luck. However, the good thing about the whole situation was *Jodi didn't care,* because why on Earth would she?

In her car, Jodi tapped on her wheel, thinking, and trying not to fall asleep. With rent sorted, the issue of Mini Wheats was top priority. Jodi couldn't stand another night like the previous and decided that she needed a crate. At the very least, in the unlikely case of a landlord visit, Jodi wanted the option of hiding Mini Wheats under the bed.

* * *

It came to her in a flash of memory from the previous day. Jodi had remembered Alpine, Rae's employee, placing a broken crate near the desk.

And now, Jodi was clambering into the dumpster behind Noah's Bark Grooming.

It wasn't stealing (*like the cans,* Jodi thought guiltily). It was, in fact, a good thing. Jodi was delaying this plastic's commute to the ocean. Plus, she already smelled ripe from sorting out old beer cans. One dumpster dive wouldn't make a difference.

Great reasoning, Jodi. Remember two years ago, when you had a well-paying job and didn't *need to depend on trash to get you through the day?*

Amongst the bags of garbage Jodi saw the crate, and was trying to find the least grimy part to grab onto when there was an angry voice from outside. "Excuse me."

Jodi wondered if staying still and quiet would convince this person she was a raccoon. Her hopes were dashed when the person continued, "I know you're in there. I'm about to call the police."

"Wait, don't do that." Jodi poked her head over the dumpster rim and met the irate gaze of Alpine. *Wonderful.* "I was just...I saw a crate in here, and figured if you weren't using it...you weren't, were you?"

Alpine's eyes flicked down to the dumpster, then back up to Jodi. "No."

"I just got a cat. And she goes nuts at night, and I figured—"

"Why were you looking in the dumpster?"

"I..." Jodi struggled. "I was looking for cans."

"Cans."

"Yes." Figuring she couldn't be more embarrassed—and not wanting to jump into the dumpster again after Alpine left—Jodi knelt down and, with a grimace, grabbed the slightly damp side of the crate and pulled it from beneath a garbage bag. After dropping it with a clatter onto the concrete, she hefted herself over the edge and fell clumsily next to it. She stood and, with as much dignity as she could muster, brushed down her mackinaw. "I am passionate about recycling. Plus, rent has reduced my account to double digies."

"You just got a cat, and you can't pay your rent?"

Jodi realized, in that moment, how perfect Alpine was for Rae. They shared a twin passion of busting Jodi's balls. "The cat is probably a stray. She was covered in fleas, and—"

"Wait." Recognition lit Alpine's expression. "You were here yesterday, weren't you? With Rae?"

Jodi held back a sigh. "Yeah. That was me. Rae was nice enough to give the cat a flea treatment." She gestured to the dumpster. "I wasn't looking for cans. I saw the crate yesterday and figured it'd be in here."

As though finally accepting Jodi wasn't a threat, Alpine reached inside the door and picked up a bag of garbage. "Rae's pretty liberal with free grooms. Hates to see animals suffer. Rae'd go out of business if enough people dropped off busted strays."

Jodi nodded. That made sense. Though a tiny, secret, shameful part of her was disappointed that her cat wasn't special. *You mean, that* you *weren't special,* a wicked part of her brain hissed.

Alpine walked over to the dumpster, and Jodi lifted the lid for her. "Don't tell anyone that, though," Alpine warned as she hefted the bag in the dumpster. "We're close enough to going out of business without chintzy pet owners taking advantage."

"You are?" Jodi dropped the lid.

"Yeah. This place was nearly dead when Rae bought it from our last owner."

"When was that?"

Alpine dusted off her hands, looking over Jodi's head in thought. "Couple of weeks ago."

"Rae's only owned this place for a couple of weeks?" *They named it "Noah's Bark" only a couple of weeks ago?*

Alpine gave Jodi a funny look. "How do you even know Rae?"

"Oh." Jodi realized how odd this situation was. Rae had made a workplace appearance with a mangy cat and an anxious woman, and the next day the woman was digging in their trash. "I'm helping with their dad's situation."

Alpine made an *oh, okay* face, nodding, then let out a small scoff. "Figures their dad would go missing right when Rae didn't need it. Sorry, I know it's awful, but still. You know."

Jodi found herself nodding, then stopped. "No, I don't. What do you mean?"

"Well, you know how much Rae hates their dad."

Jodi blinked in shock. "They do?" Alpine made a skeptical face, which Jodi took personally. "I don't know Rae that well. We only met this week."

"Oh, right." Alpine's eyes narrowed as she studied Jodi. "Weird, because you do look familiar. I thought that yesterday, too. I figured I saw you on Rae's Instagram or something."

Jodi swallowed. "One of those faces." She lifted the crate and gave it a few hearty taps, backing towards her haphazardly parked car. "I better get back to Mini Wheats—"

"Wait." Alpine's face was abruptly appalled. A finger rose and pointed, like a damning ghost. "You're Vicki Vivacious' ex."

Jodi's shaking thumb finally managed to press the right button on her fob, and her car unlocked. "No, I'm not." She opened her door and threw the dirty crate in the backseat before jumping in herself.

"I *knew* I saw you before—" Alpine's face twisted, and for a wild moment Jodi wondered if she'd have to fend off an attack. Then Jodi remembered that her car locked, and could also move pretty fast.

Jodi peeled out of the parking lot, a yelling Alpine shrinking in the rearview mirror. Jodi flicked on her radio and cranked it up loud.

"Great," she shouted over the music. "Lovely. Love this. Thanks, babe."

Well, Harper was getting what she wanted; Rae was learning Jodi's past whether she liked it or not. And as much as Jodi tried to convince herself that she didn't care, she failed. She *did* care. Because no matter how temporary this acquaintanceship was, she resented that it could be cut short by the axe forever poised above her head.

Jodi's phone rang. She tugged it from her pocket, saw *Mum,* and answered. "Hi, Mum."

"Have I got a surprise for you."

Jodi disliked the sound of that. Her mother's excitement about something very rarely overlapped her own. If their preferences were placed in a Venn Diagram, its solitary middle occupant would be macaroni salad. Regardless, Jodi upped the pitch of her voice when she answered: "Oh, cool. What is it?"

"I know you're not busy tonight, so don't even bother telling me otherwise."

Jodi's stomach sank. "How would you know that?"

"I sent a text to your friend Harper. She said you have no plans with her." Jodi's mother sounded proud, if a little shocked at her own daring. "So I took the liberty of booking us for an exercise class."

"An..." Jodi's mind whirled. "Did you book Zumba?"

The line crackled. "How did you know?"

"Because I know what you're doing— you're trying to ambush Evelyn with my presence."

"She just needs to get to know you a little."

"I think knowing me a little was the deal-breaker, Mum."

"I've talked to her since your date, and she's completely open to you being at the class."

Jodi was squeezing the wheel hard. "Yes, because she can't legally stop me from coming! Mum, I can't go."

There was a pause. "Oh." There it was— that sad, embarrassed voice that Jodi spent all her efforts to avoid.

Frantically, Jodi searched for an excuse. "I might've gone, Mum, but I actually can't. I'm..." Jodi faced the window, and her eyes landed on the distant mountain range. "Hiking."

"Hiking?" The tone was less sad and more confused. "You...hiking?"

Jodi pulled into her driveway. "I promised to go with a friend."

"Have I met this person?"

"No, they're new. Sorry, Mum. I wish I could go, but I can't back out now."

"I'm just worried about you, baby. I get the feeling you're retreating into yourself."

Jodi thunked her head on the wheel and kept it there. "I'm tickety-boo, Mum. But I have to go—need to prepare my, um, boots. And trail mix."

"Please be careful." That sad tone that Jodi hated was back. With all her heart, Jodi wished her mother's happiness could cement itself to something stable.

* * *

Harper, pale and confused, interrupted Jodi's view of the garden hose. "What the hell is that?"

"A crate." Jodi lifted the crate, emptying it of water, then continued spraying it. "I asked Evan permission to use the hose if I watered the lawn first."

Harper sat in the Adirondack chair with a groan, tightening Evan's puffer jacket around her. "Don't ask him lawn things, he has no clue. Did you get the corner behind the tree?"

"Yes." Jodi twisted off the hose. "And thanks, by the way, for sharing my sad social schedule with my mother."

Harper cranked her head up, a guilty grin on her face. "Sorry. Caught me in a weak moment."

"Well, your weak moment resulted in some backwards plan to foist me once more onto Evelyn the Zumba Instructor. The idea is that I thump around before her, sweaty and out of shape, and she'll forget abandoning a fifty-dollar sirloin just to escape me."

Harper fiddled with the zipper on her jacket. "It's not totally backwards."

Jodi dropped the hose, then slowly faced her friend. "See, the way you said that makes it sound like you knew the plan."

Again, there was that guilty smile. "We just thought it might be worth a shot."

Anger bolted through Jodi. "Seriously."

"Apparently this girl doesn't have anything against you. I told you, that first date might've just been bad meat."

"If you saw her face—"

"What harm could it do?" That open smile on Harper's face—she believed it. She really believed Jodi had nothing to worry about.

Jodi picked up the dripping crate. "So, best case scenario, she thinks *I* left *her* at the restaurant?"

"Well...yes. Which gives you an opportunity to apologize!"

Jodi turned heel and headed out of the yard. Behind her, Harper yelled, "Or, if not, you can at least explain everything—"

Jodi whirled around. "I shouldn't have to start every conversation with an explanation, Harper!"

"Then you can't be mad when dates abandon you at a restaurant."

"Oh, I absolutely can. I'm allowed to be mad." Harper raised an eyebrow, which just made Jodi angrier. "You are not allowed to lecture me on relationships, Harper White."

Harper let out a small laugh. "Well, I'm a *little* more experienced being in a relationship than you are—"

"No, you're just more experienced at being bored and wanting to cheat."

Fire lit in Harper's eyes, and she rose from the chair. Jodi took a step back, knowing she'd gone too far, but too mad to backtrack.

"I'm not going to take advice," Harper jabbed her finger at Jodi, "from someone whose screaming arguments with her girlfriend woke me up at three in the morning. Remember that?"

Jodi whirled and stalked out of the yard, stepping through the sparse hedgerow and heading to the suite's concrete steps. And there, at the bottom, was another package.

Jodi clomped down the steps, picked up the package, and hurled it away from the door. "Leave me *alone.*"

Jodi wrenched open the door, darted inside, and froze.

For a bewildering second, Jodi was positive Mini Wheats had gone on a rampage; the suite was unfamiliar in its chaos. Then her gaze hit the window near the computer. It was wide open, the pool cue lying on the ground.

A search of the entire suite confirmed, at least, that nothing important was stolen. In that time, Jodi deduced that the mess was simply the invading autumn wind from the open window scattering her pile of flyers gently over the room. Apart from that, nothing had moved.

Well. Almost nothing.

Mini Wheats was gone.

* * *

For an hour Jodi searched the neighbourhood, looking up trees and kneeling on the cold cement to check under cars. Passersby gave looks that ranged from sympathetic to confused, depending on whether her calls of "Mini Wheats" created, in their brains, images of a lost pet or of a cereal. As the search went on, sympathy overrode confusion; Jodi couldn't stop her face from betraying her and crumpling into lines of worry. Her bastard heart had gone behind her back and grown attached to the cat chirruping in a lampshade.

Jodi rounded the neighbourhood twice before seating herself on a cold fire hydrant for a break, tapping her phone on her thigh. It would help to call someone, but her mother and Harper weren't options at the moment.

Is this where I am? Only having two people I'm on speaking terms with?

At that moment, she realized that this was wrong. Currently, she had three. It would not remain three for long, but right now, she had another number to call. Technically.

The last thing she wanted to tell Rae was that she'd let Mini Wheats escape. However, they might know something about finding cats. So she tapped *call* in the contact and held the phone to her ear.

The call rang through, hitting voicemail. Jodi cleared her throat. "Hi." She cleared it again, because her *hi* sounded like she'd clocked out of a ten-hour shift in the mines. "This is Jodi. I know you're busy getting camping stuff together, but I have the tiniest question about cats, and their habits." She scratched at some gunk from the dumpster that had dried on her overalls. "But if you'd rather not call me back, I understand, and there's no obligation to text with any explanation. Good luck with your dad, and don't die in the wilderness." Jodi deeply wished she hadn't said that last part and hung up before she could make it worse.

* * *

Grey-track-suited Mr. Doucette was on the front lawn, pointing a phone downwards and cursing. Jodi—whose cat-search had yielded no results—approached her landlord. "Mr. Doucette? Is everything okay?"

"I'm trying to take a picture and the damn thing isn't working."

Jodi peeked over his shoulder and saw two things: one, he was in video mode, and two, he was recording the package she'd thrown onto the lawn.

After she told him how to get to photo mode, she asked why he was photographing the package.

"It's evidence." He jerked his chin towards the house. "I think someone broke into the suite, girl."

"Oh, well—"

"I heard a helluva lot of noise down there, right after you left this morning. Had to go into the place. Don't like doing it, but there's no way in hell someone was breaking into my house, so I went down with my bat."

The horror was mounting. "Did you find anything?"

"No. Sat down for a while, just to make sure. Opened the window just to breathe— smelled like shit down there. You sure the toilet's working?"

Jodi thought about the litter box she'd gotten with the cat food. Mini Wheats had caught on quickly, but Jodi hadn't yet emptied it. With her lackluster sense of smell, she hadn't realized how bad it was. "You opened the window?"

"Just to air it out. Went back upstairs—couldn't take the smell—but kept an eye on my window. Left to shake a tree, came back to see this package on the lawn, wasn't sure if I'd missed him and he dropped something—"

"No, no. That was me. I threw it out here." Jodi bent and picked up the package.

Mr. Doucette's bushy brows lowered over his thick glasses. "The hell d'you do that?"

Jodi shrugged, toying with a corner of the package. "It was a fit of passion."

"What is it? A bomb?"

"No, it's dental floss." Jodi held it out. "Need any? It's not a good brand, but it gets the job done."

Mr. Doucette eyed the package with a massive load of suspicion. "You're a weird girl. Just use the damn floss. Your teeth won't fall out of your head, like half of mine."

"I've got too much floss."

Mr. Doucette's enlarged eyes didn't lose the suspicion. "What are you, a *muzhik*? What's next for rent, a bag of grain?"

"No, I have rent, just...let me get the rest." Jodi sped past him and down the stairs, face red.

Jodi was frantically rolling toonies when her phone buzzed. The tension in her chest eased at the sight of Rae's name on the screen.

Jodi tucked the phone between her shoulder and ear as she gathered her motley pile of money. "Thanks for calling back, I just had a question."

There was heavy breathing, then a throat clear. "Shoot."

She paused. "Are you okay?"

"Why do you ask?"

"I'll explain in a sec." Back outside and up the stairs she went, where she gave the money to Mr. Doucette and purposefully avoided his reproachful gaze when the toonie roll hit his palm. Jodi hurried back down the stairs. "You sound weird. Tense."

"You got that from a single word?"

"So you aren't okay?" Jodi struggled to work a shoe off.

"To be honest, I took a little fall."

Jodi froze, shoe half off. "Off a cliff?"

"What? No, not off a *cliff*. I was using an old wooden ladder to reach something, and the legs collapsed."

"Are you hurt?"

"My ankle is a little swollen."

"You broke your ankle?"

A heavy sigh crackled the phoneline. "Will you stop increasing the severity of what I say? I said it was *swollen*. Probably just strained."

"Can you stand?"

"I haven't tried yet. I've been sitting here, fuming."

Jodi sped into her bathroom, her single shoe slapping. "Do you want me to bring you some bandages?"

There were some shuffling sounds, and a low gasp of pain. "No, that's fine."

"Why not? I'm not doing anything." Jodi rummaged in her drawers, locating a tangled mess covered in dust and cobwebs.

"Having you bring medical supplies is a bit too friend-ish."

"I'm not doing it as a friend. I'm doing it because I feel bad about you giving Mini Wheats a free groom."

There was a *thump* on the other side of the line, and a soft gasp of pain.

Jodi stuffed the bandages in her bag. "What's the address?"

"It's really not necessary—"

"Shut up." Jodi hung up, feeling empowered. Then she sheepishly brought up their contact and hit *call.* "I, um, still need the address."

* * *

Jodi was nervous seeing Rae's home without their wholehearted permission—it was like visiting their work, only worse—but reminded herself that Rae hadn't had the same anxiety when infiltrating her bathroom. Then she pulled up to the townhouse, saw the massive pile of wood next to the door, and realized that this home wasn't even Rae's.

For a moment she debated knocking, then shook her head and twisted the knob. She poked her head inside and sent a tentative "yoohoo?" into the darkish hallway.

"In the garage," came Rae's voice.

Jodi closed the door behind her and edged down the hallway, which was taken up by a huge plastic kayak. The house smelled like kerosene and celery and had the unvacuumed feel of an owner whose top ten priorities didn't include house management.

In the messy garage, which seemed to function partly as a pantry, Jodi found the splintered remains of a very old wooden ladder and, sitting next to it, a very dejected pet groomer.

Jodi pulled the wad out of her bag. "I found an assortment." Kneeling on the ground next to Rae, Jodi started to untangle the ball.

Rae felt the material of an end. "This one isn't even a bandage. It's boxers' hand wrap. What the hell do you have this for?"

"It was my dad's, though he didn't box either." Jodi glanced down at Rae's socked foot, which to their credit was elevated on a box of crackers. "Do you want to wrap it yourself, or do you want me to do it?"

The awkwardness hung in the air. "Uh..." Rae crossed their arms. "I guess you could, if you know how."

"I can figure it out."

"Exactly what patients like to hear."

"Can you pull your pant leg up?" Rae did as Jodi asked, and she took a moment to study the foot. The ankle was red and indeed swollen, with blueish bruising starting to spread. "Are you sure you don't want to just go to the hospital?"

"I'm not up for a five hour wait."

As gently as she could, Jodi wrapped the foot with the bandages. Rae kept sniffing, which Jodi took for an attempt to hide the jolts of pain. Jodi didn't have the most delicate touch—she was too fumbly to be delicate.

When she shifted to get a better angle, she noticed a tattoo just under the ankle bone. A teeny cartoon. "Aw. Shark."

"Yeah. Shark."

"Why?"

"Gives something for dachshunds to look at."

Jodi grinned. "Is that the real reason?"

"No, I made that up. Real reason's because I was eighteen, and thought sharks were cool. Was my dad your only client?" Rae's voice was strained, but their tone was curious.

Jodi wondered if this was a shot at her having time to play doctor in the middle of a workday. "I have some steady work doing short-form videos with a few social media marketing managers. But your dad took—

takes—up a big chunk of my time. He's my biggest client."

"Sorry about the abrupt halt in funds."

Jodi nodded, not sure if they were making a wry joke. As horrific as the situation was, it didn't erase the grim reality of Jodi's unreplenishing bank account.

"I'm losing money too," Rae continued. "Just opened my own place, and I can't even work."

"I understand. It'd be hard to work right now."

"No, I'd much rather be at work. But I can't." Rae huffed a sigh. "He's my dad. I can't do a thing until I know I've tried everything to find him. Even if it means losing the place I'd worked my ass off to get."

"You're a better person than me."

Rae jerked their head to the side, and Jodi wasn't sure if they were disagreeing with her or spasming in pain. "You're here. Stop with the self-deprecation."

Jodi glared at them. "I'm not being self-deprecating. I'm saying I literally would not have done what you're doing. If my dad was lost in the woods, I would've just let the professionals look." She sighed. "Or maybe I wouldn't have, I don't know. Too late to find out now."

"You have a bad relationship with your dad?"

Jodi jerked her shoulder. "No, not bad. Just...not good. We both went through the motions of having a father-daughter relationship, but it was never genuine. He never really liked me much.”

“Past tense?”

“Yeah, he kicked it three years ago.” Jodi reached the end of the bandages and held the end. “I don’t know how to finish this.”

“You don’t have those little...” Rae gestured something indiscernible with their hands. “Metal things?”

“No.” Jodi gazed into the middle distance. “I wonder...”

“If you say something about twine I’m going to lose my mind.”

Jodi whirled, surprised. “Now how did you know I was thinking about twine?”

“I guessed. You’re not wrapping my foot in twine.”

“I wasn’t going to.”

“Yeah, because you probably don’t have any in your car.”

Jodi stood, furious. “Stop assuming things.” She was feeling very nettled; being observed was not an activity she was terribly fond of. To hide her nettlement she wandered the lower floor of the house until she found a bathroom. In there, she searched the drawers and cupboards, finding an impressive variety of items that were completely useless to her, and also useless in a bathroom. In a drawer was a butter knife, a Lego man, and several old-fashioned Christmas lightbulbs. On a shelf was a grungy soap dish—no soap—a plastic Garfield cup, and a very old BC Hydro bill.

Eventually Jodi located two Band-Aids that weren't just the discarded wrapper and returned to the garage, where she did her best to affix the end of the bandage in place. Rae waved away Jodi's proffered hand to help them up, and instead opened a cabinet drawer—filled with a shocking amount of supplement and pill bottles—to assist them in standing, and once vertical they tested putting weight on the foot. They nodded, and Jodi was hopeful. "How does it feel?"

"Awful. Hurts like hell." They leaned heavily against the counter, their expression stormy. "This is going to make camping a real gas." They gestured harshly to a can lying on the counter. "All because I wanted what I thought was a flashlight but ended up being a can of garbanzo beans. Why he keeps his food in the garage, I have no idea."

Jodi didn't know what to say. *"You can wait a few days to go"* was useless—Rae was feeling every second as it painfully passed. *"The trip is a fool's errand"* was also not good.

"Anyway, I appreciate the bandages." Rae bent down and grabbed a backpack off the floor. It clanked with what Jodi assumed were various bits of camping equipment. "You should get back to Mini Wheats."

The name caused a cramp in Jodi's stomach. She didn't want to mention it, not anymore. There was nothing Rae could realistically do—Jodi had just wanted to talk.

In response, Jodi faked a smile. "If you need Ibuprofen, just give me a holler." She hitched her bag on her shoulder.

Rae waved a casual hand. "Nah, I'll be fine. Why take Ibuprofen when I have…" Rae glanced in the open pill drawer and pulled a bottle out, squinting at the label. "Deer antler velvet." Their nose crinkled slightly, and Jodi could practically see the words *what the hell* floating above their head.

Jodi, to her own surprise, giggled. "I've heard of that. I think there's estrogen in it."

Rae chucked the bottle back in the drawer. "Yeah, and he probably has another pill with an equal amount of testosterone. If you added up all those pills, with his luck, they'd cancel each other out with mathematical precision."

Jodi couldn't tell Rae's tone. Was it fondness or frustration? In her ears rang Alpine's voice. *Rae hates him.* She wondered just how true that was.

* * *

Late that afternoon, Jodi skimmed a non-uploaded early draft of a video in the same campsite Grant had gone missing from. It wasn't likely the same spot, but regardless Jodi kept a watchful eye for any information the searchers hadn't noticed.

To her surprise, she did notice something. It was within a trudging walk to the beach that Grant made Jodi remove for the final video, because the camera's anti-shake function wasn't working in the low light, and he was nauseated watching it. In the shaky footage, she noticed a sign on a water spigot, and was able to make it out after zooming and lightening.

It was nothing. But she wanted to send Rae *something*. Some kind of result from this useless footage before their trip. So she sent a screenshot.

As she waited for a reply, a gust of wind whistled through the cracked window. With a rock in her gut she tightened her mackinaw around herself.

The image of Mini Wheats, with her bony back and pieces of missing fur, wouldn't leave her brain.

Another gust of wind blew in, and she watched it rustle the pile of posters she'd printed the day before. Making up her mind, she grabbed them and stood.

* * *

Wrapped in her blue mackinaw, Jodi was taping twine to a poster when her phone buzzed, finally, with a reply.

I don't remember seeing this.

Jodi leaned against the post and tapped a reply. *In an exported draft I forgot to delete. Did the searchers know the water spigot was out of order?*

I don't think so.

What if he needed water? He'd have to drive to a specific parking lot, according to the sign. Have they looked at this lot for any clues?

I don't know.

You should check there for clues.

I'm not going.

Jodi stared at those words. Relief was immediate—more profound than it had any right to be. *Why not?*

It took them a bit to reply, so Jodi resumed posting. The paper would be destroyed two minutes after the rain came—and there was rain in those distant clouds—but she didn't have any way to laminate. She just hoped the pre-makeover photo of Mini Wheats was recognizable enough. It hadn't occurred to her to simply reprint with updated information until after she'd spent twenty minutes with a Sharpie replacing "FOUND" with "LOST."

Twine instead of staples. Unlaminated posters. Wrong photo and caption. Searching for a cat that she couldn't even keep. Everything about this was off. Regardless, Jodi headed for the next post and whipped out the twine.

Her phone buzzed.

I can't drive with this foot. Could barely press the pedal enough to get home today.

Sorry the trip is off.

All good. It wouldn't have resulted in anything.

With the dogged determination Rae hadn't yet strayed from, Jodi found the indifferent tone of the text hard to believe. There was nothing she could say—a sprained ankle wasn't healed with a perfectly worded text.

Then, suddenly, her phone lit up with an incoming call. Immediately she answered, tucking the phone between her ear and shoulder. "Hi."

"What's it like having a dead dad?"

Jodi snipped off a piece of twine, but just wrapped it absently around her fingers. "Empty."

"Yeah?"

She rested her forehead against the cold wood of the post. "There's that big, Dad-shaped hole. But when you aren't close, that hole feels emptier than it should be." Jodi's stomach clenched with guilt. "And that emptiness just gives room for guilt to seep in." Jodi closed her eyes. "So, guilty. I feel guilty."

"Why weren't you close?"

Jodi clenched her hand, the twine tight and pinching. "He never wanted a daughter. I was always kind of off-putting to him, I think. Too flabby, too soft, too...wet. I cried a lot. He wanted a tough boy to be tough with and he got this squat girl who didn't even have the courtesy to be good-looking."

"Excuse me?"

"And the funny thing is, as I got older, I could see he wasn't even a tough guy. He was this businessman who once hurt himself on the punching machine at the arcade." Jodi let the twine unwind from her fingers and rubbed the indents left behind. "See, this is my bitter side. Because some days we'd play cribbage, and we'd laugh together. And as far as the Dad Olympics go, he wouldn't have been disqualified. Just never on the podium. So, I feel confused. And guilty. And empty." She realized who she was talking to. "But you shouldn't be thinking about that."

"Why not?"

"Because you're supposed to be optimistic."

"I'm sick of being optimistic." Rae heaved a sigh. "I want to go back a week, when my biggest problem was the sheer amount of stuff I own."

"I get that. I've been pawning my life on markets online to get some extra cash—my place is getting minimalistic, but in a poor way. Are you sentimental?"

"Nope. Just have a really tiny apartment—had to downsize to afford the business. Tons of shit has to go—I've got this gigantic old record player cabinet from my grandparents' that I climb over to get into my bathroom. Bit sad, but also, why in the hell do I have a hemorrhoid pillow?"

"For your hemorrhoids."

"It wasn't. My dad bought it second-hand as a birthday gift."

"Why?"

"I don't know. I never knew. He's just unpredictable. Could've just been because he thought it was funny, but could've also been referencing some slight I'd forgotten about."

Jodi continued walking. The sun was a sliver behind the mountains, and leaves rustled along the cold, red sidewalk. "Rae..."

"What?"

"It's okay to have hemorrhoids."

Silence filled the phone, and Jodi was embarrassed that she'd even attempted a joke. Then a truck drove by, close enough to the sidewalk that Jodi instinctively leapt backwards onto the grass. Her foot slipped, and she tumbled to the ground, phone and posters scattering around her.

Rae's tinny voice emitted from the dropped phone. "What just happened?"

She picked up the phone. "I fell down...dropped my posters..." They were everywhere. Some lay in the ditch, Mini Wheats' grainy photo soaking up old, filthy rainwater.

"Are you on the road? I heard a car. What posters?" They paused. "The ones about Mini Wheats? I thought you were keeping her?"

"Good frigging Lord, pump the breaks on those assumptions, would you?" Jodi sighed, then explained the whole situation, hoping Rae wouldn't judge her. "And I just thought, even if she wasn't *my* cat, I'd still put the posters up. Just so she doesn't..." She swallowed. "Go to a shelter, where they'll take one look and think, nah, she's got no owner, she's ugly as sin, she's not worth saving—"

"If she's found, they'll bring her to my grooming salon."

Jodi blinked. "What? Why?"

"I put a collar on her, remember? It has our information on it. I'll text Alpine, make sure she knows to contact me if someone calls or brings her in."

Jodi pressed a fist to her forehead. "Oh. That's...good to know." A lump was in her throat, and she hoped her voice wouldn't crack. "How did you know to do that?"

"I keep a few collars on hand in case an animal doesn't have one and I'm worried about them escaping. Are you crying?"

Jodi swiped at her face furiously. "I told you I'm an easy crier. You shouldn't point it out."

"It's not a bad thing to cry."

"I hope not. I'm the human equivalent of a wet dishrag." Jodi swiped her cold, running nose with her wrist. "Thanks for putting the collar on her. And for talking. I've had a bad day."

"Me too."

"Are you sure you're a person who doesn't want to make friends? Because this is a friend kinda thing."

"I'm in my thirties. I've got more friends than I can handle."

"So like, one or two?"

"Yeah."

That hurt, a little. But Jodi merely smiled and jerked a thumb at herself, as though Rae could see through the phone. "Haven't got this one, though. I'm a great pick—I never go out, and fifty percent of the time I'm a drag to be around."

"Tempting." Rae yawned into the phone. "You should get back home. It's getting dark. And I need to elevate this stupid pissant foot."

"Rae, your foot isn't going to determine whether or not your father is found. You know that, right?"

There was a grudging silence. "Can't say I tried everything now, though, can I? One stone is unturned, all because of an expired can of garbanzo beans."

Oh no.

Jodi felt it.

That horrible little instinct that told her to help.

Don't do it. You like your warm home and your kettle and your heating pad. Don't do it don't do it don't do it don't—

"What if I drove?"

Idiot.

* * *

See, this was the thing.

Jodi's brain had only absorbed the drive.

The *getting there* part.

It also vaguely envisioned her whacking in pegs at Rae's direction, unloading the bins of food and equipment, and enjoying a cup of coffee after a hard evening's work. After that, her brain had auto-populated her end-of-day as, somehow, being in her own bed, warm and safe.

The logistical flaws presented themselves, one after the other, on her walk home. They came in time with her steps. *It's an hour drive. You can't just leave Rae there with an injured leg and no car. You have to stay the night. There is only one tent. There is only one BED.*

Well, she could remedy that—except it involved talking to Harper, which wasn't a palatable prospect. Still, if she was facing potential death by bear, she should tie up loose ends anyway.

On Harper's stoop, she waited for her knock to be answered and planned what she'd say. They'd both been hurtful. Despite this, Jodi still resented being the first to apologize.

But Jodi wasn't proud enough to stay in a fight. The feeling of someone's anger was poison; it permeated her body and made it sick.

The door creaked open, and Evan yawned at her, lizard-blinking. His thinning blond hair was rumpled, and he was tugging down a hastily thrown-on shirt. "Oh, hi…"

In an act of mercy, Jodi cut him off from attempting to remember her name. "Hi,

Evan. Sorry—did I get you out of bed?" It was only seven, but Jodi knew he often got up early for pickleball.

"All good, all good. Here for Harper?" Jodi nodded, and Evan scratched his head. "Sorry, but she's out with a girlfriend tonight."

Jodi tried to remember what other women were in Harper's life. She, Jodi, wasn't jealous—but it sure made her own life seem sad.

"Anything I can help with?" Evan smiled dopily, clearly half-asleep. It wasn't a bad look. Jodi was well aware of Harper's frustrations regarding her husband, but Jodi knew they were empty threats. Harper was a fan of the fantasy, and dearly wished her life was more dramatic than it was. Perhaps it was good for her to have Evan, a man eternally brushing aside anger with a mild grin on his face.

"I was actually wondering if you had an air mattress I could borrow, in exchange for a few days of lawn-watering."

Evan retrieved the mattress, relieved to be unhooked from lawn duty. "She has this special way of watering that I can't seem to get right." He passed the folded pile of plastic to Jodi. "Just make sure you bring it back. Never know the next time I'll get kicked out of bed."

"Oh. Is there a chance you'll need it tonight?"

He whisked a hand around. "No, no. She's staying over at her friend's. A girls' night. So I get the bed all to myself." He pumped a fist, then affixed Jodi with a sympathetic look. "I'm surprised you're not with them."

"That's fine. I don't even know Harper's other friends."

"Oh, you probably do."

Jodi knew this was a thing that bothered Harper to no end. Evan's self-assuredness at things he didn't know—especially things about his wife. *Oh, you like pickles. Come on, you've been to the East Coast, I'm sure of it.* Still, Jodi felt bad watching him strain to remember this girlfriend's name, though somewhat relieved his bad memory was not just limited to Jodi.

"Jodi." Evan looked proud. "That was it. Like Jodi Foster. They were going to Zumba, then having a slumber party."

"Ah." Jodi nodded, her smile forced for several reasons. "Great."

After Evan closed the door, Jodi sat down, once more, in the Adirondack chair, clutching the folded air mattress. There was irony in her name being remembered only when it didn't apply to her, that was for certain. But it wasn't her main concern.

What are you doing, Harper?

Jodi was in on the secret now. Whatever Harper was doing, Jodi was involved as an alibi. The man behind the door was blissfully unaware of anything amiss, thanks to his own lack of care in knowing his wife's friends.

"I tell you to stop, you tell me to stop, that's the deal."

If Harper were here, she'd demand Jodi talk her off the ledge of a bad decision. It's what Harper had grown to expect. Jodi would stop them after two cans of Colt 45. Jodi would, in her rare social moods, stick like glue to Harper in a bar, eyes locked on the drinks. Jodi would run after Harper and pull her back gently.

Harper would knock on the door and cut through the screaming, saying to stop, to calm down. She'd take Jodi out of the house, away from Vicki, who was crying on the couch, coiled up into a knot around her phone.

To Harper's credit, she still remained Jodi's friend after that night, and everything else that followed. Harper seemed to find comfort in Jodi. And Jodi always wondered if it was because Harper held a secret relief that, even if her worst moments were broadcast live, she'd garner more sympathy from viewers than Jodi ever would.

People forgive cheaters. They don't forgive abusers.

Jodi's finger hovered over *call* in Harper's contact, knowing what it'd result in. An evening starring Harper. She may even be waiting for Jodi's call. Expecting an apology for their earlier fight and preparing to announce what had happened in Jodi's absence. Jodi envisioned sitting with Harper in a 24-hour McDonald's, listening dutifully while she talked through her guilt, or anger, or euphoria.

Jodi exited out of Harper's contact.

Not tonight.

Jodi didn't have the time. For the first time in a while, she had something new. Something not yet connected to her sticky, fetid past.

She had the opportunity to be eaten by bears.

Chapter 6

They drove into the evening, the sun low in the sky. Jodi didn't like driving, especially in rain, and was warily eyeing the incoming clouds. It had been clear for weeks; it was like they'd waited for the very moment she decided to leave her heating pad.

My chair would never get in an accident that'd leave me smeared over the pavement like last week's jam.

Nevertheless, she kept quiet as Rae gave directions. The car had already been packed when Jodi arrived, sporting her little backpack filled with mainly socks (a good fifty percent of Grant's videos featured him announcing how wet his feet were). Rae had "packed all essentials," and Jodi didn't ask questions, despite knowing it was a risk. She didn't know Rae well enough to categorize them into the two-party system of "person who prepares for daily diarrhea" and "person who forgets to pack underpants." Still, Jodi intuited that Rae was the former, simply to balance out their father. Like the pills in Grant's drawer, the two of them cancelled each other out.

Jodi hoped she was driving smooth enough for Rae and their tender ankle. She'd noticed their driving before. Cautious, jaw set, despite sitting relaxed in the seat. Eyes flicking to check the mirrors. Like they really understood the weight of the machine, and how easily it could kill someone. Jodi had appreciated it. Had felt, surprisingly, safe.

Eventually the wider, built-up town and city streets gave way to narrow single-lane roads flanked by thick forest. It was surreal, seeing it in person. Jodi had only seen this route on her screen.

The longer they drove, the more Jodi imagined them travelling down a long green hallway that narrowed the farther they went. There was something secretive about it. They were leaving their own world and entering Grant's. Entering the mountains that had swallowed him whole.

Jodi realized that she hadn't told Evan where, exactly, she was going. Hadn't told anyone.

It would be a while before people connected the dots, especially if Harper's lie about a girls' night with Jodi slowed things down. Then Jodi and Rae's names would be inked after Grant's on the long list of people swallowed.

Relax, Jodi told herself, after noticing just how hard she was gripping the steering wheel. *People camp. It's a normal, mostly safe, family activity that only sometimes ends in disaster.*

It was pitch dark. Jodi stepped out of the car, the cold hitting her skin and immediately plunging her mood to the bottom of her stomach. With just over an hour of driving, they had travelled into November.

This was the weather she endured in parking lots in the walk between her car and a warm building. This was not weather she stayed and slept in, surrounded only by a paper-thin bit of nylon.

Grant was a *lunatic*.

With a sigh that billowed out before her, she rounded the car, where Rae was getting out. "Do you need a hand?"

They waved her away and limped to open the trunk. "We have to set up fast. I don't want to kill the car battery leaving the lights on." They pulled the tightly bagged tent out and dropped it with a *clank* on the cold dirt.

Jodi rotated, taking in their surroundings. Perhaps in daylight there would be a view through the trees, but right now they were surrounded by gelatinous shadow. "I can't see your dad going into those woods at night." Jodi tightened her mackinaw around her, which she had supplemented with several fleeces. "I have no idea why he'd move camp." She knelt by the tent bag.

"He wouldn't. Not unless he had to."

Jodi set to work with numbing hands, snapping the tent pole together. The videos didn't do justice to just how finicky the whole operation was, especially when her fingers stopped cooperating.

"I can't figure this out." Rae was struggling with the stove, which was in pieces. "Nothing fits." They held up a piece to the car's headlight, squinting.

"It probably fits, just not very well." Pole constructed, Jodi set on unfolding the tent shell. "Grant always complained about warping from the heat, remember? Just have to force it."

"I'm worried it's just wrong. He didn't use this stove—maybe this was why."

Jodi shook her head. "It's just bigger. He only uses it in the coldest weather."

Rae continued attempting to slot the pieces together. "It's weird."

"The stove?"

"You, knowing my dad. How he thinks."

"I don't. Not really." Jodi shook out the crumpled tent shell like a bedsheet on the dirt. "His unpredictability is why we're here."

They worked quietly for a minute. Then: "Why did your friend call me Shit Hawk?"

Jodi's cold face was, suddenly, blazing hot. "Sorry."

"Is it because of—" Rae tapped their nose.

Jodi was mortified. "No! Well...I don't know. I didn't ask. But I'm pretty sure part of it is because you took a shit in my toilet before I even knew your name." Jodi stood up straight, her back stiff. *When did I get old.*

"Oh, I never used the bathroom."

Jodi froze mid-back-crack. "Excuse me?"

"I was looking around. Seeing if my dad had been there."

Rae continued to struggle with the stove while Jodi stared. "Why would you think that?"

"He worked with you."

"Why didn't you just *ask*?"

The stove collapsed inward, and Rae huffed in frustration. "Can we just continue putting this stuff up so we don't freeze?"

Aggravated, Jodi continued spreading out the tent flat. She'd already felt foolish for letting a stranger into her house; now she knew it was deceit after all. Not *awful* deceit, but still a lie, and not to mention her least favourite thing—being judged on sight. Their first meeting was laced with suspicion, which was somehow worse than their first meeting being baptized with a coffee-induced bowel movement.

Jodi dropped the side of the tent and marched over to Rae. "So what, you thought I'd killed him?"

Rae's surprised eyes hit hers. "What? No, I thought you were sleeping with him."

Without meaning to, Jodi let out a strangled yelp—half laughter, half gag. "Excuse me?"

"What?"

"How on Earth did you come to that conclusion?"

Rae sat back, a confused dent between their thick brows. "He likes younger women. He's a charmer when he tries, and some girls like that rugged, dwarvian look he's got."

"Why would you think *I* did?"

"How would I know you didn't? For a video editor, you've got a pretty sterile social media presence. No relationships. No photos or videos, other than a really outdated picture of you on a job search website. You looked so trusting and wide-eyed. At the time, I figured you'd be the type to get..." They struggled to find a phrase. "Sucked in."

Jodi didn't have a leg to stand on. She *had* gotten sucked in. Not by Grant, either. Rae had managed to coax her out of her nice, warm suite and into freezing, bear-infested forest. *And they weren't even charming.* "You don't know me at all, Rae Marlowe. My lack of social media isn't because I'm inexperienced, it's because I hate it. And I am not one who gets *sucked in*. In fact, I'm the one who—" She stopped, just before saying *sucks*.

Rae's mouth twitched. "You're the one who...?"

"No, I'm not going to say it."

"An assertion that passionate must be concluded."

"I don't have to do anything. And I *don't* like being laughed at, so wipe that grin off your face and finish putting together a simple stove before next frigging year." She whirled and went back to the tent, which the wind had panini-folded.

* * *

The setup took over two hours and went as smooth as gravel. The chimney didn't roll properly, the guy lines were tangled, and the ground was so cold and rocky that seven of the twenty metal pegs bent under the inexperienced whacks of Jodi's hatchet back.

It was when it began raining that Jodi reached near hysteria. A drop landed on her neck just as the hatchet back hit her thumb for the eighth time, leaving the peg sideways in the dirt. A screech of frustration rent the darkness.

"Want me to take a whack at it?" Rae, unable to help without a second hatchet, tried to light the area better with their phone light.

"No, I'm getting used to it."

"I should do it. It's my dad." Rae raised their voice. "Would be great if he wandered out of the woods, right now, and saved us the trouble."

"He'd just point out what we were doing wrong." Jodi's teeth were gritted as she aimed the hatchet for her aching thumb. "'*Now* that's *not it*,' he'd say, with great joviality."

"Don't forget *Danny Dewitt. That's not it, Danny Dewitt.*"

"He calls other people Danny Dewitt? I'm disappointed—thought it was a personal nickname."

"Nah. Just a collective name for people who do things wrong."

This is everything you hate, Jodi thought as she attacked a peg, her knees aching, her hands frozen, her back damp. And yet, despite her misery, she wasn't technically hating it—not completely. Maybe because someone was with her, feeling just as miserable.

In the end, the tent itself was lopsided and not as tight as Jodi remembered from Grant's videos. However, it was standing, and it shielded the nearly frozen pair from the biting winds and rain. Unfortunately, they still needed to make a fire, and chopping kindling was a chore with Grant's ironwood. Jodi almost lopped off Rae's good foot when the hatchet glanced off, and they finally confiscated the tool.

"Did you bring fire starters?" Jodi was searching the plastic bins.

Rae looked up from their own inexperienced hatchetry, forehead gleaming with sweat. "What?"

"Fire starters."

"That's what the kindling and matches are for."

Her heart sank. Rae detected her mood—or perhaps they just noticed how her face crumpled. "What? I've never used fire starters, and I've built plenty of fires."

"With hardwood? In the cold?"

Rae's mouth thinned.

"Grant never built a fire in the cold without a fire starter—"

"Oh, he didn't, did he?" Rae snapped. "Pardon me. I forgot that his methods worked out great for him, with nothing ever having gone wrong, ever."

There was a long silence in the tent. It was the most silent silence Jodi had ever experienced, even with the rain. Never had she realized just how much highway traffic soundtracked her life. "I don't know how your relationship is with your dad," Jodi picked at the rim of the plastic bin, "but he's my sole reference point for this entire process. And I'd rather not be on eggshells when I mention him."

Rae put down the hatchet and rubbed their eyes. "Sorry. That was rude."

"It's fine."

They dropped their hand and appraised Jodi. "It'd help if you weren't already on eggshells."

"I don't like camping."

"I didn't mean just now. I mean always." Rae reached into their pocket and pulled out their phone. After a moment of tapping, they held it up and snapped a picture.

"What are you doing?" Jodi's heart knocked against her chest, and she threw a useless hand to block her face. "Delete that."

Rae flipped the phone. "This is you, always. You've got your mouth downturned, and the ol' wrinkled brow going full tilt, every time I see you."

Jodi knew it. Not in mirrors—she tried her best in mirrors—but on video, she always looked worried. "Can you delete that, please?" The sentence bounced in her head, an echo of the past.

But to her relief, Rae nodded, and tapped *delete*. "You're uncomfortable with photos." They said this slowly, as though just realizing it. "Why?"

Jodi bit her lip, not wanting to have this conversation. Why did she even have to? Plenty of people hated being photographed. It was rarer to find someone who liked it.

And so, she avoided answering. "This seems more like a friendship conversation. We're not friends, remember. We're just..." Jodi pondered. "Camp buddies."

Rae sniffed a laugh and returned attention to the wood. "Camp buddies need to talk, too. There's nothing else to do in this godforsaken tent."

"It's like me asking why you've got issues with your dad."

"Plenty of reasons." Rae gathered the small splinters of wood into a pile.

"That's not an answer."

Rae piled the wood in the stove, then appraised Jodi with a searching gaze. "If I tell you one thing about that, will you tell me one thing about your hatred of pictures?"

Jodi didn't like that. But Rae said one thing—not everything—and so she nodded.

Rae set to work constructing the kindling in the stove into a tiny, burnable structure. "One thing I remember is bringing home my first girlfriend. It was Thanksgiving, and I was nervous. My dad's unpredictable. Never knew if that day he'd get pleasure from being charming, or from saying something offensive under the guise of a joke. My girlfriend was perfect—standard thoughts of a twenty-year-old—and I didn't want her getting scared off. And I was still wanting that approval from him. I wanted the two to get along." Rae shook their head hard, as though displacing a memory stubbornly stuck.

"I can only imagine what Grant said."

"Oh, he said nothing. Thanksgiving went fine. But Christmas Eve my girlfriend broke up with me, and I found out later that she and my dad had slept together."

Jodi gaped at Rae. "On Thanksgiving?"

"No. It was a month later. On November eleventh."

"On *Remembrance Day?*"

"Yeah, so now that's wrecked for me, too."

Jodi didn't want to think about Grant that way in any capacity—again. "I don't think you can wreck Remembrance Day."

"Oh, yes you can. Moment of silence, and all I can think about is my dad's flabby ass."

Jodi winced. "What's today's date?"

"September...nineteenth, why?"

"You've ruined September nineteenth for me."

A blast of wind shook the tent, and the conversation was cut short by their tandem realization of how unlit the stove was. Thus began their attempts to light the fire, none of which worked. The dense, cold wood refused to catch. Jodi was planning on panicking until Rae reminded her that, if all else failed, they could just drive home.

For a shining moment, Jodi imagined leaving. But she couldn't let her hope show on her face, no matter how useless she found this trip.

Rae limped outside to gather some other materials that might light better, while Jodi continued with the matches. Ten minutes later, unease enveloped Jodi. Rae was taking too long. Rae had gone, alone, into the woods that had eaten their father. And she'd just let it happen.

"Rae," she said softly, then louder, "*Rae.*"

She dropped the box of matches and scrambled out of the tent. "RAE."

There was a crack, and she whirled around. Relief untensed her gut as her camp buddy limped from the treeline with a handful of forest debris and a baffled expression. "I think that took ten years off my life. What's with the screaming?"

Jodi darted to their side, as though the shadows of the woods would reach out and yank them back. "You shouldn't go into the woods alone, you frigging fool. And you were taking forever to find seven twigs."

"I have a *sprained ankle.* I walk at the speed of a newborn."

"Yes, exactly. You're beginner prey—you're what mother bears tell their cubs to catch."

Rae stared at her. "What, were you worried?"

Jodi drew back. "No. Die, for all I care."

Back in the tent, Rae unloaded the debris next to the stove, then turned to Jodi with a concerned frown. "You didn't try to light the stove with gas, did you?"

"What? Of course not."

Rae blinked, then shook their head. "Thought I smelled gas. Never mind."

* * *

Jodi decided, that night, that she was entirely correct.

Camping was awful.

It was cold. So cold. The tent was wide, but teepee style—the only place Rae could

147

stand straight was in the centre. With the dirt floor, there was nowhere to sit except a knotty bit of hardwood each. Food that should take twenty minutes to make took an hour. And she'd been forced to use an outhouse that made her—despite the very real danger, darkness, and indignity of it all—consider squatting at the mossy stump of an ancient Douglas Fir the next time nature called.

"How is it," Jodi flung aside the tent flap and scooted inside, edging around the stove that partway blocked the door, "humans looked at the concept of *vacation* and decided to see how many forms of suffering they could pack into it before people just stayed home?" Compared to the outhouse, the tent was roasting. She had to give the stove that credit, at least.

Rae added more oil to the tiny pan on the stove, which was filled with pre-chopped vegetables. On the ground was a wrapped and thawed steak Rae had found in Grant's freezer. "So the outhouse was fun?"

"No! There was no toilet paper! I had to sit there and drip dry while this enormous moth smacked against the wall." Jodi sat down on her piece of hardwood. "And then I kept thinking about Grant disappearing in this same exact spot, and I could barely muster the courage to leave the outhouse." Jodi shivered and adjusted her block-chair. "When your dad shows up, I'm increasing my prices for editing until I feel properly reimbursed."

Rae unwrapped the large steak from its wrapper and, after making room within the vegetables, laid the meat into the pan. "Let's be real here. My dad is probably dead."

The steak's sizzling filled the tent. Jodi was speechless. *What happened while I was in the can?*

"That's the logical answer, right?" Rae poked the steak, moving it into the shimmering oil. "He left food in his tent at night and got pulled into the woods by a bear, or fell into some hole and broke a leg in the freezing cold. I know that."

"But, his stuff—"

"Probably stolen. The tent and stove are expensive. Makes sense they'd leave the wood, leave other stuff that they couldn't carry."

Jodi stared at Rae. They'd said everything so matter-of-factly, like they'd stated the obvious. Like the silence and solitude of the campground allowed room for their mind to stretch out, to tentatively feel the possibility it had been avoiding.

And then she saw something at Rae's feet. A dirt-covered can of bear spray.

Rae followed her gaze and tapped the can. "Found that in the boxes. I assumed he had it on him. Said he always did."

Something told Jodi this wasn't the time for pity—Rae would brush it away. And so, instead of comfort, instead of the well-meaning sympathy she was sure Rae had dealt with for weeks, Jodi said, "Did you come to this conclusion before or after I had to drip dry in a moth-infested outhouse?"

Rae blinked at her. "Do you go to funerals with that unbelievable level of compassion?"

"Yes. People hated me there, too."

"Oh, shut up. No one hates you."

Jodi huffed in exasperation. Then, to her own surprise, she reached out and turned Rae's face with her finger so she could meet their gaze. "Yes, some do. Stop assuming you know me just because of a very short glance online."

Rae's head didn't move from the position Jodi had put it in. Their expression didn't change, save for something in their eyes Jodi couldn't decipher. She'd just wanted to scold this companion of hers—camp buddy, but not friend—for falling into that same irritating habit of assumption that Evan had, but was it common to hold a gaze this long? Only now was she noticing how dark Rae's eyes were.

Vicki's eyes were grey. The colour of November sky. Vicki had liked that they were grey and had gotten irritated when Jodi once called them blue. *They aren't blue. There's no colour, see? It's actually rarer than blue. Less than one percent of the population.*

Where'd you hear that?

Online.

Vicki always had her phone on her, and not just for posting. She was constantly checking facts. Jodi was often wrong about things, and it became a joke between them. Vicki hated being wrong. She'd sulk until a way to twist her original opinion into the right one occurred to her, and all would be well again. Eventually it became too tiring, and Jodi would resign herself to being wrong every time. It kept Vicki happy, which made Jodi happy. It was only an issue when Vicki found Jodi's mistakes funny enough to document.

Jodi tore her gaze away, picked up the spatula and—not knowing what to do with it—poked the steak in the pan. Rae watched her wordlessly.

"I need you to have hope." Jodi patted the backside of the steak. "Because if you don't, then I'm missing a night with my heating pad for nothing."

"God forbid." Rae pulled out their phone and directed it at the pan, taking a photo of the steak, then at the surrounding tent. "Need proof I did this. Alpine wouldn't believe me otherwise."

Jodi drew her hood over her head. "Don't get me."

Rae lowered the phone. "Are you in Witness Protection or something?"

Jodi knew she had to say something. She'd promised, after all. "I don't like pictures because my old girlfriend loved filming me. Specifically when I was doing something wrong. If I broke something, or said something stupid. That kind of thing. If you searched her phone, you'd think she was dating a moron with no motor skills." Jodi poked the steak again.

"You can flip that."

Jodi inched the spatula under the steak and flipped it, revealing the golden underside.

"Is that why you looked weird when I explained the *We Did Do That Here* wall?"

Jodi jerked her shoulder. "For you guys, it's harmless. It just brought up some uncomfortable memories for me."

"Your ex sounds like a real grade-A asshole."

Jodi honked a laugh. "You might be right, but it's hard for me to say."

"It was showing her flaws more than yours. Documenting the bad, and never the good."

Jodi hadn't thought of it that way. Again, she poked the steak—she was acutely aware of how much she depended on her phone to busy her hands. "One good thing about your dad—he filmed everything. Bad, good. Never wanted anything taken out."

"Oh, believe me, he'd delete clips he didn't want you to see. Or, if he couldn't figure out how, he'd just avoid giving you the SD card. He can be sneaky. And he likes to look good for the ladies."

Jodi was becoming more and more aware of that disdain Rae felt for their dad—

or maybe they'd stopped hiding it. "I don't think your dad cared much about being suave in front of me. I've seen many a video of pee hitting his shoes, and I've listened to countless farts."

"He thinks that's charming, Jodi."

"Lord." Jodi gazed at the steak. "I admire it. I'd be a lot better off if I cared as little as he did about messy bits captured on film."

Rae nodded. "It's a good thing I didn't film you using that hatchet. Or attempting to comfort the grieving."

Jodi threw them a filthy look. "Lighting a fire. Putting together a stove. Getting something off a shelf without falling like an old person."

"Driving at the speed limit."

"Driving at all."

"Finding a cat."

"Finding a *dad*."

Jodi slapped a hand over her mouth, horrified until Rae sputtered a laugh, and she joined in. The two of them were laughing hard enough to break the too-quiet silence, hard enough to mask the sizzle of the slowly burning steak.

The stove was earning its keep. The tent was toasty now, to the point where Jodi was able to remove her coat. The steak, while overdone, was indeed food, and disappeared fast. Jodi had never seen Rae eat before and found herself staring. It was normal (the eating, not her staring) but it was always interesting to see how any person ate.

That's what she was trying to convince herself of, anyway. The truth was, Jodi wasn't able to go long without looking at her camping buddy.

And why not? Why am I not allowed to look?

Suddenly it felt as though Harper were in the tent with Jodi, a scolding look on her face, and Jodi was on the defensive. She could imagine what her friend would say. *You're not ready for this. And even if you were, this is not the kind of person you need.*

Jodi never was sure what kind of person Harper had in mind. It was almost like Harper imagined no one. Jodi was better off with no one.

Then, from outside the tent, there was a scream.

Chapter 7

Jodi's hand was clutching Rae's jacket sleeve. She didn't even remember reaching for it. Rae, in turn, had grabbed the back of Jodi's fleece and yanked her off her log chair and closer to them. Their jaw was tense, eyes wide, listening.

After a few quiet seconds, Rae whispered, "It must have been—"

Jodi never found out what was coming next—bird? racoon?—because, again, a scream cut the night.

It was a word this time, though. *Fuck*. A man was screaming *fuck* in a way that must've torn at the throat, but he just kept going, over and over.

"Is it Grant?"

"No. That's not his voice. Sounds like someone on drugs."

"How far away is he?" Jodi took a bite of food, but it went down in lumps.

"Not far." Rae's eyes were still on the tent's zipped-up door, as though expecting it to tear open. "A few campsites over."

Jodi had thought the tent walls were thin before; now it was all she could think about. How penetrable and bright, with the ostentatious fire-glow inside. It wasn't any shelter at all, really—if anything, it was a neon sign stating: *Disposable income! Rob and murder here!*

Jodi pushed her paper plate into the garbage bag. "I think we should turn in. I don't like how obvious our tent is."

They cleaned up the tent, which involved the nervous task of taking their food and garbage to the car (Jodi would take a beating from a crazy man over a Grizzly tearing their tent open) but eventually they faced the task of preparing to sleep. Unfortunately, not even a man's blood-curdling screams could distract from the palpable awkwardness.

It took some maneuvering to fit both beds around the stove. Rae offered to take the blowup mattress and allow Jodi the comfort of the raised cot—which was slightly broken, but which Jodi had mended gleefully with the twine and tape she'd brought along—but Jodi declined. The rainwater had seeped in and made little pools on the dirt floor, but as long as it didn't rise more than six inches, she'd be dry.

A worry also had been the lack of privacy in the tent—no room to change—but that, too, had an easy solution; it was so cold, they didn't bother undressing. In their preparations for bed, the fire had died down, and Jodi's nose was running with the cold.

Rae switched the final battery-powered light off, and the darkness was complete.

Never before had Jodi seen nothing so completely.

And yet, all other senses were working overtime. The strange, plasticky-oil smell of the tent and Grant's spare sleeping bag overwhelmed her, and under that was the wet, woodsy scent of outside. She was cold, and the constricting sensation of being fully dressed in bed wasn't great. The trees overhead made the rain fall in huge, heavy drops on the nylon tent, and every once in a while, *"FUCK."*

She didn't want to say anything, though. It felt wrong to complain. Unnecessary. The last thing Rae needed was her groaning her way through a favour.

Then, Rae's voice floated through the pitch black. "Is this how you imagined spending your Thursday?"

Jodi thought for a moment. "I never imagined going to bed with socks on. That part's a surprise."

"I never go to bed without socks."

Jodi rotated, the air mattress squeaking a symphony, until she felt pretty confident she was glaring in the right direction. "I beg your absolute pardon?"

"Keep your feet warm."

"That's what the blanket is for, you Martian."

"The ladies love it."

"The ladies have been *lying*."

Rae's soft laugh was barely discernible over the rain.

"Is it to cover your ankle shark? Does he take away from your aloof veneer?"

"I think my aloof veneer didn't survive the socks-in-bed. And no, I like my shark. It was my first tattoo."

"How many do you have?"

"Six. You?"

"None. I'm indecisive. What's the one on your chest?"

"Lighthouse on rocks. It's my biggest—goes down to my stomach."

That put the image of Rae's bare chest and stomach in Jodi's head. The only thing she could think to say was, "That must've been itchy."

"Oh, it was a nightmare." Rae was quiet for a few moments. "I wish my dad wasn't lost in the frigging woods."

Jodi was relieved they'd gone back to classifying their father as *lost* and not *dead*. "Yeah, I know."

"I wish we weren't here *because* my dad was missing." The rain was loud on the nylon. "I wish we were just here."

Jodi didn't know what to say to that. Of course, if it wasn't for their very missing father, Rae would've needed duct tape and rope to get her out here recreationally. But Jodi was more so focused on that *we*. That Rae was thinking of the two of them outside the confines of this nightmare.

"*FUCK.*"

Just for a moment, Jodi imagined that Grant, suddenly, waltzed alive and well out of the forest. What would it mean? Rae had been very clear that this was a professional, non-friendly relationship, and no wonder. Who wanted to remain connected to a person so entwined with a nightmare?

But they said they'd like to.

Jodi hadn't held onto many friends. As adulthood trudged on, her school friends dropped away, and in the last two years her inbox was barren, save for the too-frequent insults and death threats. Her only friend, really, was Harper—and she'd remained likely because it was hard to drift from someone living next to you.

This lack of friends was partly Jodi's fault. She'd retreated inside, physically and mentally, and hadn't made the effort to hold onto anyone. It was partly exhaustion, and partly pride. *Why should I make the effort? Why don't* they?

She'd been stubborn. It was easier to fade than fight, even if it meant her final image was a bad one.

Now, she couldn't help but wonder what Rae saw.

Jodi was not used to being seen as just her. Jodi, with no past. And even though Rae seemed prickly and aloof and uncharming...they were here, saying that they'd like to camp with her, recreationally.

Jodi hated camping. But suddenly the idea of coming back wasn't quite as nightmarish. Not if the idea involved Rae. Even if it included a horrible man yelling profanities into the darkness. He, at least, had faded, like a passing thunderstorm. His shouts had given way to silence as he wandered out of the campsite.

Jodi spoke into the void. "Do you think your dad would leave if he met someone bad here?"

"Like a crackhead?"

"Like a criminal." Jodi shifted, the bed squawking again. "They use campsites as dumping grounds for stolen cars and stuff. Grant talked about it once. Do you think there's a chance your dad had a run in with some bad guys?" Her brain filled with images of Grant attacking hardened criminals with a block of ironwood.

"I'm sure it's been there as an idea, but I'll bring it up to the searchers." Rae's tone was hard to place. "But even if anyone...did anything bad, and hid Dad somewhere in the woods...it's still a body that hasn't been found."

They fell into silence. The wind rustled the trees, and Jodi pushed images of tree limbs falling onto the tent out of her brain.

Then, Jodi felt a tickle on her cheek. She worked her hand out of the bag and scratched her face, and her fingers touched something. Something spindly and very awful.

Then, on her neck, another tickle.

Jodi sat bolt upright, grabbed her phone, and tapped the screen to life. Rae let out a yelp as the tent was bathed in light, and

Jodi could see with horrible clarity the many, many things that were on her.

The noises she made weren't screams, necessarily, but only because she spent her lung energy on getting out of the sleeping bag. She did let out very strangled howls, which Rae mirrored in twin panic. *"What is going on?"*

"SPIDERS." Jodi stood, wobbling, on the mattress, slapping at her body. Goosebumps erupted on her skin from disgust and cold. "So many, so fucking many—" She lost her footing and fell, yelping, back onto the mattress at an oblique angle. Her hands and one socked foot hit the dirt, splashing in the puddles of dirty water.

Rae scrambled for their own phone and put on the proper flashlight. They made a sound in their throat. "Come on here, they won't come up on the cot—"

Jodi scrambled next to Rae, still swiping at her arms and body with wet hands. "Why, oh why—"

"The heat. They're taking shelter from the rain and the cold." Rae was checking their own bed. Apparently, Jodi's proximity to the still-warm stove—and the ground— made only her a target. "Do you want me to grab your sleeping bag?"

"Rae, I can't stress enough how *filled with spiders* it is." Jodi realized the issue as she was speaking and her teeth chattered, but she would freeze to death before she touched the cursed bag again. She was imagining the heat-seeking spiders marching into the warm inside. The absurdity was making her giggle.

Rae was fighting not to laugh now. "I don't think those are spiders—daddy long legs, more likely—"

"Oh, well in that case, let me get *right* back into that sleeping bag." Jodi yanked her wet sock off and threw it onto the infested air mattress. "Stupid *sock*." She was breaking her "no complaining" rule but didn't feel at all bad about it. She drew the line at being covered in *fucking spiders*.

Rae shifted. "I guess..."

"You're gonna take the spider bag?"

Rae let out a sputter. "Are you insane? I'm not touching it."

Jodi understood, in a very explosive epiphany, what Rae was going to suggest. It was the only suggestion, barring leaving. And as much as the idea of leaving called her, like a siren song, she was too exhausted to even imagine packing up, let alone driving in the rain and darkness in unfamiliar backcountry.

Still, she never would have suspected a day ago that the solution to the problem of "too many spiders" would be sharing a bed—nay, a *sleeping bag*—with Grant's uncharming child.

Of course, the cot was about as wide as a cupboard shelf. It took some struggle until both realized it was pointless to find a chaste position and resigned themselves to the only workable arrangement: Jodi's back pressed right up against Rae's chest.

Despite the cold, Jodi's face was ember hot. "Sorry."

"It's fine." Rae's voice crackled. "I'm the one who should be sorry. I took you from your nice warm bed into a place where the only shelter from crackheads and Grizzlies is a spider-infested sack."

"To be fair, you couldn't have predicted the spiders."

"No one predicts the spiders. It's a rule we'll tell the aliens when they invade."

"They'll still be stuck on the confusion about camping being voluntary and not a punishment. I keep reminding myself that we're supposed to find what made Grant pack up and leave the campsite, instead of finding a reason he came in the first place." Jodi had a thought. "What if he left because of the spiders?"

"If he was squeamish about spiders, he'd just go home. The woods are full of them."

"I don't think so. Not anymore. I think they're all in this tent." She adjusted her head, and the pillow squeaked. She froze, then poked it. "What is this pillow, Rae?"

Rae said nothing.

"Rae."

"I didn't know I'd be sharing it."

Jodi squeezed her eyes shut. "Ew, Rae. *Ew.*"

"I never used it."

"It was *used*. Why would you bring a used hemorrhoid pillow to sleep on?"

"It took up less room." Rae was laughing now, which set Jodi off.

It dispelled some of the awkwardness, but not the physical discomfort. Jodi didn't move, though she was desperately squirmish. Despite the several layers—and three socks—between them, Jodi was very aware of Rae's skin beneath it all. She wondered how uncomfortable Rae was. They didn't seem like a touchy-feely person, outside of touching animals.

"Do you want me to sleep in the car?" Jodi whispered.

"Hm?" Rae seemed distracted. "Why would you do that?"

"I don't know."

"You're weird. Go to sleep."

"Well, I'll take a while to sleep, and I might fidget. I haven't slept in a bed with someone in a while, and never smooshed right up next to them."

"Don't care about the fidgeting. You're not sleeping in the car. It's where the food is—a bear could rip the door off."

"Oh." That wasn't a fun thought. "Y'know, if we got eaten by a bear, no one would know. I never told anyone where I was going." She could imagine the analysis videos now—"*Jodi Marples is the last person who would embark on a camping trip. Tonight, we're going down the rabbit hole on Jodi's disappearance, and why she lied about the trip that would erase her from the world forever..."*

Rae didn't speak for a second. "You know, I don't think I did, either."

"You didn't tell Alpine?"

"Why would I do that?"

"Isn't she your friend?"

"Alpine is a work friend. I don't talk to her in my spare time."

"I think she likes you."

"I hope not, for her sake."

Despite Rae's certainty, Jodi wondered if Alpine had elected to contact them with a warning about Jodi. Perhaps the text was there, sitting in the limbo of un-delivered messages, waiting for the moment Rae came back into service. Perhaps it would be a block of text, or a simple link.

The logical solution would be to head it off at the pass. Explain now, so Rae got Jodi's side first. It was the way to go, but Jodi still couldn't do it. Explaining was like fighting for her life, and she was tired of it. So, instead: "There's this Christmas song I really like."

Rae sat with that for a moment. "You know, I don't think I could've predicted that being the next thing you said."

"The vibe is about talking to baby Jesus and outlining all the crap he'll go through in adulthood, but for now he can sleep. I like the idea of procrastinating misery. That even though things are going to be shitty later, right now your bed is warm and you can put off worrying.”

“Are things going to be crappy later?”

“Just...thinking about Mini Wheats. That’s all.”

The wind rustled the tent. “You got a weird email, the first time I went to your place. When we were looking through the videos, before you kicked me out.”

Jodi’s brain flashed back to the moment that email notification popped up. How she’d clicked it away a couple seconds late. “I thought you didn’t see that.”

“It made an impression. Someone saying that you shouldn’t exist. It seemed weird.”

“People say weird things.”

“Yeah, but that you shouldn’t exist? Very weird.” Rae yawned. “Like, I could see them saying you were annoying.”

“Great. Thanks.”

“I was just thinking of this week. How it would’ve gone if you didn’t exist.”

“And?”

“It would’ve been a week where my dad was missing.”

A confused reply was on Jodi’s tongue, but then she understood. It wasn’t *just* a week where their dad went missing. Jodi had wormed her way in, breaking up the nightmare.

She smiled into the hemorrhoid pillow. “If you didn’t exist, I would’ve been sitting bored and miserable in my suite, my only bit of excitement being my neighbour's moles and her desire to have an affair."

This threw Rae for a second. "Because...of the moles?"

"No. Well, kind of."

"...like, she has cancer, and it's a Make-a-Wish thing, or...?"

"What? No, critter moles. Moles in the ground." Jodi pulled a face. "That would be an unpleasant Make-a-Wish."

"I didn't know people planned affairs. I thought that was something that happened on impulse." Rae's tone was sour, and Jodi recalled their story about Grant and the girlfriend and Remembrance Day.

"Apparently not." Jodi could almost see a shape in the darkness. The barest hint of lighted ember in the stove. She focused on it. "I thought she was kidding, but she's out with someone tonight. She's going to be mad I wasn't there to stop her—I'm her bounce board and her bouncer."

"Too bad my dad wasn't around. He's always up for a nut-n-bolt."

Jodi rotated slightly so she could look at the darkness that contained Rae's face. "You'll have to let that go, for your own sake."

"Never. I'm going to resent him for it until I die. It's healthy."

"Is it?"

Rae's somewhat joking tone dampened. "He doesn't think of the world outside the one in his head. That's what bugs me. His reasoning was that he'd done me a favour, that I wasn't prepared for someone like her. In reality, he just saw a pretty girl." Jodi felt Rae shake their head. "One time, he thought about life outside himself—he was a little drunk and told me to listen close, because I needed to learn something. Cue this story about this old homeless woman he saw on the street and how, despite looking like a broken train engine—his words—she might just consider herself the most important person in her own world. He had this look on his face, like he expected me to have that eureka moment alongside him, like realizing I'm not the only person on Earth wasn't something I figured out during naptime in kindergarten. You know, I've been a groomer for seven years, and not a visit goes by where he doesn't ask what I'm doing these days. I think it's on purpose. Reminding me of my place in his life. Had a grand opening for my own grooming salon, and he couldn't even cancel a camping trip."

Jodi let Rae talk themselves to silence and took a moment to answer. "The going missing bit is kind of rude, in context."

"Isn't it, though." Rae let out a sigh that ruffled Jodi's hair. "I'll have to let this stuff go, won't I?"

"Probably best. But I am sorry."

"This doesn't leave the tent, by the way. It's bad timing to be bitching about Dad."

Jodi's eyes were fixed on the ember. "Don't worry. This trip exists in a liminal plane. The world thinks we're at home, safe in bed, and we're more than welcome to go along with that narrative come tomorrow."

"Eager to forget this happened, are you?"

Jodi smiled. "No. Not at all. But the rest of the world doesn't need to know about it. Isn't that neat? It's just ours."

"You want it to be ours? Even with the mothy toilet and the spider sleeping bag?"

"Have to take the bad with the good."

"You're the most positive miserable person I've ever met, you know."

Jodi wasn't sure if that was a compliment. "I don't know why you think I'm miserable."

"Because I can sense it. You're not happy."

Even within her million layers, Jodi felt naked, and stared hard at the ember. But this night wouldn't exist tomorrow. "Would you believe this is the happiest I've been in a long time?"

"No."

"Well, you're going to feel like a real moron when I say it's true." Jodi sniffed. "Hard to believe, considering I'm hanging out with someone who recoils at the idea of being my friend."

"I don't recoil at it."

Jodi let out a *pfft*.

"No, it's...can you turn for a sec? I don't want to talk to your hair, it keeps getting in my mouth."

Embarrassed, Jodi twisted around. Her eyes had adjusted so that, just barely, she could see the outline of Rae's face.

"I don't think I could be friends with you."

This felt worse. She was no stranger to being told unkind things, but it hurt worse when it was someone new, who only knew her at face-value. It hurt to be told that friendship with her wasn't worth the time. "Fine. I get it. I don't think I could be your friend, either."

Jodi twisted away again. A moment later, she felt bad for being petulant. Rae obviously wasn't keen on keeping connections with people they met due to a family tragedy.

Still. "Actually, no, I don't get it. I might be miserable and annoying, but I'm really low maintenance, friend-wise. I'm really bad at texting back, so you could ignore my existence anytime you wanted. You're giving up a great opportunity here."

"Jodi."

"What."

"You're also really bad at reading between the lines. I'm saying I couldn't *just* be friends."

That shut Jodi up for several long seconds.

Her brain, suddenly, was making a low frequency buzz, like speaker feedback, and her stomach squirmed.

Then: "You'd want to be business partners, you mean?"

"Jesus—"

"No, I get it." Jodi's heart pounded hard. Her blood was rocketing through her veins and the disorientation was bad, and she wondered if this feeling was normal. Perhaps she was having a heart attack. That would be bad timing. "Why is, um…why is that a bad thing, to you?"

"I wasn't saying it is."

Jodi twisted around. "You've just barely met me."

"I know that. But you're pretty easy to read, and I know me well enough."

"I don't think I'm—"

"It also means now would be the time to say it's a dead end. You know. Before it gets worse."

"It?—"

"These past few days, I keep getting distracted from my possibly dead father by thinking about you taking your coffee into the bathroom for some reason, or insulting a stray cat to comfort it. And if I'm not thinking about that, then I'm thinking about the smell of your shampoo, or the freckles on your hands, or how you keep biting your nails, but gentle enough so they don't fray— like you're just giving them a warning. So tell me now if I should, you know, nip this in the bud." Rae's tone was cool and unbothered— same as usual—but Jodi knew now their tell.

The words came faster, and it was hard to break in with words of her own.

Jodi's head was spinning as she recounted the last five days. How many hours within them her brain drifted to the stranger who'd broken (basically) into her suite to shit (allegedly) in her toilet.

But that was her. It was more her style to develop a crush. Vicki had been delighted with how smitten Jodi was and gave love like a gift. Like it was something Jodi deserved, and sometimes—sometimes—didn't deserve. After everything ended, Jodi had wondered just how much Vicki had actually loved her, or if she'd just loved being loved.

Jodi was used to following like a lovesick puppy. Rae's confession—as vague as it was—hardly seemed real.

Still, Jodi had to answer. So she did, stumbling over uncharted territory. "I...I wouldn't suggest any nipping."

"All right."

Jodi and Rae lay there, in that liminal space of theirs. In that space, Jodi felt a flicker of hope. Slowly, she wormed her hand around until it found Rae's, and she carefully laced her fingers in theirs.

Jodi didn't know what to expect next. She didn't know if they would have gone to sleep like that, or if their hands would pull apart after that brief connection. She never found out, because out of the blue, Rae said, "Are you sure you didn't use gas in the stove?"

Jodi blinked, disoriented. "What?"

"I'm not going to be mad if you did. I hope you know that."

"I didn't use any gas, Rae. Why are you asking?"

"Because I keep smelling it. It's driving me nuts."

Jodi shook the haze from her head and sniffed around. She couldn't smell—wait. "I kind of smell it. A bit. But my nose isn't that good."

Rae was sniffing around, and Jodi's face flushed when they got close to her face, her hair. Finally Rae raised their connected hands. "It's this. Did you pump gas earlier?"

"No." Jodi pulled her hand from Rae's and sniffed her fingers. Indeed, there was a faint gasoline smell. "Maybe it was in the equipment."

"I would've smelled it when I was packing."

Jodi was flummoxed, thinking back on what she'd touched. The outhouse, perhaps. The borrowed air mattress—had Evan spilled gas on it?

Then, in a flash, she knew. "My hands hit the dirt when I fell over. It's the ground. There's gas on the ground."

"Someone must've parked here at some point, or brought a jerrycan to use in the fire pit. Spilled some gas in the dirt." Rae paused. "For fuck's sake. That's it."

"What?"

"That's why Dad moved."

Chapter 8

In total, Jodi got around an hour of extremely bad sleep. Aside from the discomfort of the cot and their rigid, awkward positions, the previous night's conversations ran through her head at rapid speed, and the adrenaline spike of the spider scare, and her own frazzled emotions, kept her heart thudding heavily in her chest until the wee hours of the morning.

The moment the first light peeked into the tent, Rae spoke. "Are you awake?"

"Yeah."

"Did you sleep?"

"A minute here, a minute there. You?"

"No. Can we get up now?"

"Yep."

Jodi unzipped the bag, and the two of them sat up with dual groans. Jodi twisted from side to side. "My bones are crispy crunchy today. I can't wait to reunite with my heating pad. How's your ankle?"

Rae tested it, standing gingerly. "A lot better, actually. Sleeping here basically iced it for twelve hours."

They decided to relight the stove before packing up. Neither was hungry—the lack of sleep had made them nauseated—but coffee was necessary if Jodi was expected not to crash the car. The two of them didn't speak as Rae chopped up some new kindling and Jodi stacked it into the stove. The awkwardness from the night before hung in the tent like the humidity already did—condensation dripped down the tent walls.

Jodi kept glancing at Rae, expecting them to talk first. Their face was unbothered, bored—like always. Though, their admitting to Jodi being on their mind had made her reevaluate that look. *Did Rae really say all that?* It seemed unbelievable in the morning light. Perhaps she'd just dreamed it in her meager minutes of sleep.

Rae made cowboy coffee, stirring in some grounds they'd brought in a baggy into the metal mug of water heated on the stove. There was no filter, so Rae poured some cold water over the grounds to help them sink, and the pair took turns sipping the strong, grainy brew. The words *our first coffee date* flashed through Jodi's brain like a breaking news ticker tape, and she choked on a bitter swallow. Even as she sputtered, she couldn't help the warmth that flared in her stomach.

Rae surveyed her over the rim of the metal mug. "Are you dying?"

She whacked her chest. "Nope. Fine." *Charming. Remind me why I like you, again?* "So, just to recap, you're thinking Grant moved his tent in the middle of the night because the ground smelled like gasoline?”

“If that smell was there when he was—and I’m willing to bet it was even stronger—I would bet money on it. The man’s olfactory system is as fine-tuned and sensitive as a CAT scan. I have some very humiliating memories of him insisting my friends showered when they came over because the smell of other people’s homes drove him nuts—that sure made me popular in middle school.” Rae offered the cup. “Last sip?”

“No, I think I’ve had what I can handle.”

Rae threw back the last of it and chucked the metal cup into a box. “Let’s go.”

The two of them exited the tent into the cold, damp morning and walked to the mouth of their site. “What’s your instinct?” Jodi asked, glancing both ways.

Rae thought for a moment. “Left.”

They went left and walked/limped down the gravel path until they reached the neighbouring site. “Do you know if anyone checked these other sites for clues?” Jodi walked over to the wet picnic table.

“Probably not.”

The campsite was empty, save for a chocolate bar wrapper under the table that both agreed wasn’t Grant’s—he hated caramel—and decided to leave that site be, instead heading for the neighbour on the right. That site, too, had no evidence that pointed to Grant.

Rae was looking dejected, so Jodi forced her tone to be positive. "Let's go left again. Go to the next one. He wouldn't have liked the first one."

"Why do you say that?"

"The ground was sloped. He hated it when his bed was sloped. He needs even ground."

They backtracked, passing the first site, and heading to the next. That ground, too, was not very level, and the two of them decided to continue to its neighbour.

Rae surveyed the site. "This one is level."

Jodi was bent over like a hunchback, studying the ground as she walked, when she spotted something. "Rae, look at this." She pointed excitedly.

"Holes?"

"Peg holes." She tracked her finger along the ground. "Could be for any tent, I suppose—"

Rae darted forward and scooped something off the ground, sniffed it, then indented it with a thumbnail. "Bit of ironwood. He was here."

The two of them searched the area meticulously. Other than the piece of wood, the site was clean, but Jodi refused to sound disappointed. "At least we know something new." She searched the picnic table once more, even looking underneath, which did nothing but reveal an unfortunate plethora of gum. "We can tell the police. Also, we still need to check that parking lot where the spigot is, there definitely might be—” The words died on her lips. Then she got on her knees and crawled under the table towards something lying in the dirt.

She picked it up and scooted backwards. Standing, she brushed off her wet knees, then walked over to Rae, who was poking in the wet ash of the fire pit with a stick. Into their hand Jodi pressed the little baggy, then lifted her arms in celebration.

Rae studied the baggy and, for a moment, couldn’t place what was inside. Then their face went blank with shock. “You’re kidding. You didn’t just find this.”

“It was under the picnic table. Must’ve fallen through the slats.”

Rae stared at her. “You’re not kidding?”

“No, jeez, why would I?”

Rae’s face broke into the first real, uncool smile Jodi had seen, and before Jodi could process it, she was off the ground. Rae was swinging her around like a ragdoll.

“Be *careful*,” Jodi yelped.

“I’m not going to drop you—”

“Drop me all you want, be careful with the card!”

“Oh. Right.” Rae set her down gently, and Jodi plucked from their hand the baggy—in which was the tiny micro SD card—and slid it into her mackinaw pocket.

* * *

The drive home had an entirely different vibe than the drive there. Success made the roads smoother, the traffic lighter, the air sweeter. Jodi was unable to keep the smile off her face. It was unbelievable, the joy she felt from doing something right. From being a positive force in someone's life.

Rae was keeping up a string of conversation, mainly one-sided, going through all the possibilities of what could be on the card. "Of course, it could be blank. Or corrupted. Who knows. But I'm guessing, if the thing was out of his camera bag, that it was a card he'd filled and forgot to put back. And it's in a baggy, so I doubt much moisture got in. I didn't see any drops inside. There's also the very real possibility that nothing of use is on there at all—that it's just the first part of his trip—but any look into what he was feeling or doing on the day he went missing is potentially useful..."

Almost absently, Rae reached for Jodi's hand and squeezed it. Jodi's whole body was warm. It had been a while since she'd felt so warm.

* * *

Harper's car was back in the driveway when they got to Jodi's. Just its presence threatened Jodi's mood, so she put it out of

180

her mind as they headed down the cement stairs to her door. No packages on the stoop—the day was getting better and better.

Inside, Jodi put on the kettle for proper coffee, then booted her computer. Carefully, with Rae watching anxiously over her shoulder, she opened the little baggy and tipped the tiny card into her palm. It was dry, thankfully, so she slotted it into her card reader, said a little prayer, and plugged it into the computer.

Immediately, the little window popped up, and with a grin she clicked "open folder to view files." And there they were—a long list of video files, filling up the entire 128 gigabyte card.

Rae shook Jodi's shoulders in barely bottled excitement. "Can we look at them?"

"Let's transfer them first. I'd rather they be safe on my computer before we get lost in the videos."

After making a new folder, she copied the files and watched as the little progress bar began its sluggish journey. Satisfied it was working, Jodi returned to her kettle, which whistled happily, like it shared her good mood.

As she went through the process of brewing the coffee, she let herself zone out. Her exhaustion from lack of sleep was there, but buried under layers of excitement— about the chip, about Rae, about...well, about Rae. Rae, listening intently to her musings. Laughing at her jokes. Holding her hand, shaking her shoulders, admitting that she was the kind of person they'd fall in love with.

Jodi hadn't necessarily envisioned dying alone. However, any daydreams she had about finding someone were tainted with thoughts of half-hearted singles nights and blind dates and the repetition of her favourite colour. She'd assumed any partner was going to take work to find—like embarking on an archaeological dig, except any bones found also had the ability to abandon her at a restaurant.

But she hadn't found Rae. They'd found her. And it was easy.

She hadn't imagined easy.

She filled her coffee with cream and sugar, and her eyes fell on the second mug. She didn't even know how Rae took their coffee. There was so much she still had to learn about this person, but it didn't feel like work this time. With a smile, she picked up the mug and returned to the workspace. "Are you a cream and sugar person, or do you hate fun?"

Rae, leaning against the desk, was looking at their phone, brows knitted. "That's fine."

"Not really the answer I needed." Jodi tilted her head, confused. "Everything okay?"

Rae jerked their head, eyes still on their phone. Then they looked up, and...

Jodi's chest clenched, and her ears rang.

There it was.

She could have imagined the look away—that familiar shocked look—but from Rae's phone came that voice, words Jodi knew by heart, which played in her brain on the worst of robe days and, conversely, whenever she'd allowed herself to get too happy.

She'd allowed herself to get too happy.

When, oh when, would she learn.

And just like that, the wall came down. Jodi straightened up. "Who sent that to you?"

"Alpine." Rae bit their lip, face ashen. "This isn't you, is it?"

The words cut into her skin. They were binding her, forcing the air from her lungs. And yet, still, she was unable to let loose all the words she stored inside. Words that she desperately flung at closed ears, back in the beginning, when she still had hope. "It's me." Jodi waited. Her brain screamed at her to *say something, idiot,* but her stubborn, hardened pride simply waited.

"There are so many views..." Rae swallowed. "Why didn't you say anything? Why did I have to learn about this from my *employee?*"

"Sorry. There was never a moment to bring it up."

"There were a lot, Jodi."

"Let me rephrase: there was never a moment I *wanted* to bring it up." Jodi was shocked at how cold her tone was. She wasn't speaking to Rae, not wholly. She was speaking to everyone now. Every person in her life, and every tiny person behind every comment under the video on Rae's phone screen.

Rae was speechless. Then they shook their head hard, as though clearing it.

"Alpine was probably pretty thrilled to be the person to tell you." Jodi was clenching the mugs so hard they were burning her hands.

"No, she was worried. She'd sent a text before we left, and it didn't come until we were in service. Why would she be thrilled?"

"People love spreading things like this. Being the one to educate, inform, warn, all that."

"I'm sorry, are you actually angry at Alpine?"

"I'm angry at her, and every single person who ever liked, or shared, or even looked at that video."

"So me. You're mad at me."

"Depends."

"On what? Because all I'm feeling is disoriented. All week I hang out with a girl who cries over a stray cat and drives twenty minutes to bring a stranger bandages, and on this screen is that same girl in a very, *very* viral video, with millions of views and tens of thousands of comments, *beating her girlfriend.*"

Jodi was frozen for a moment. Then she forced the words out, words she'd said before, many times— "It's not what you think. It...there's a lot of things going on there—"

Rae scoffed. Maybe they didn't mean to, but it came out, nonetheless. That little exhale and head turn that meant, *Yeah, okay. Sure.*

This flared rage Jodi hadn't felt in a long time. "Oh, great. Right away, huh? Not even going to let me explain."

Rae indicated with the phone. "Explain this?"

Jodi was frozen for a moment. Then she put the cup on a table, hard. The coffee sloshed over the edge and onto her hand. It hurt—badly—but she barely registered it as she strode to her desk and, with enough presence of mind to make sure it wasn't still transferring, ejected the SD card. She pulled the chip from the reader, dropped it in the baggie, and pressed it to Rae's chest. "Take this and go."

Rae stared at her, hand holding the baggy to their chest. Then, after several long moments, Rae left the suite, closing the door hard behind them.

Chapter 9

The coffee got cold as Jodi sat on her lumpy couch, staring at the window jammed shut by the pool cue. Her hand ached, having been burned by the coffee. In fact, her whole body ached. It seemed incredible that not two hours earlier, she had been walking on air. Now, she'd sink in cement.

Almost like someone else controlled her, Jodi picked up her phone and navigated to Vicki's account.

Jodi had visited the page a few times over the last two years. There was never any good reason why she kept looking—it was always a force outside her that dragged her in.

Video after video. Vicki was popular— she'd gained so many followers during the course of their relationship. She was so unbelievably beautiful, and smart, and goofy—followers adored her. At first Jodi had wanted nothing to do with the online life, but after a while Vicki had convinced Jodi into filming, then faceless cameos, then full-face, and soon enough their relationship was a large part of the channel.

Jodi never wanted to look at the videos, too self-conscious to see what millions of people already saw. Not until one day, she received a nasty comment on an old account of hers. "Someone said I was being shitty to you," Jodi had told Vicki, showing her the comment.

"People are idiots." Vicki had wrapped her arms around Jodi's neck and kissed her temple. "There's always the crazies when you're famous."

She always went into soprano when she said the word *famous*. Jodi usually laughed, but not that time. "Maybe you should stop posting me. People are probably sick of my face."

"I am *not* stopping. People love seeing us. Forget you even saw that, I'm serious. And I'd turn off direct messaging. I did that already."

Jodi obliged, but despite Vicki's assurances, Jodi could never get that nasty comment out of her head. One day, she went to her girlfriend's channel and found that her account was blocked from seeing the videos. The alarm bells went off, so she made a new account and tried again.

There were more videos now since she'd looked that first time. Videos that started off sweet—relationship challenges, days-in-the-life, makeup tutorials—but got more and more ugly. Jodi watched herself transform on screen. Arguing, sullen silences, yelling. Screaming.

"You know I hate this fucking floss."

That was a bad one. The first one where Jodi had been physical.

Even now, two years later, Jodi didn't look at all of them—she never could—and instead went right to the one Rae had seen. Jodi forced herself to watch it all the way through, and by the end her face was wet, and she was breathing hard, bile in her throat.

The house was suffocating—she needed fresh air.

The air wasn't as cold as it was at the campsite, but it was still crisp as she walked up the damp cement steps and through the hedge into Harper's backyard. As she crossed the lawn, she saw with confusion that the mole traps had been pulled out and were lying next to the ragged holes. At the door, she was about to knock when the sound of yelling made her pause, knuckles an inch from the wood.

The familiar sound made her gut tense, and so she sat down in the Adirondack chair and waited. Eventually the sound stopped, and—as Jodi knew would happen—Harper pushed open the back door and came outside, wrapping her cloak around herself and stopping short when she saw Jodi.

Jodi studied her friend. "Is everything okay?"

Harper bit her lip, then gave a jerky shrug. "Can we just like, go walk somewhere?"

The two women circled the neighbourhood. Jodi recalled her walk the day before, putting up signs about Mini Wheats. How, despite her worry, her heart had beat fast when Rae called.

"Evan takes me for granted."

Jodi broke out of her misery to stare at her friend. "What did he do?"

"Nothing. That's the point." Harper jerkily tucked a lock of hair behind her ear. Her makeup was smudged, but it was a full face—she hadn't removed it from the night before. "I'd married a charming, athletic guy who bought flowers and took me seriously. This man hasn't bought me flowers in years, and just tunes me out. My worries are second to a pickleball game. Then I do something, and now he chooses to pay attention. *Now*. Not when I needed him to."

"What did you do last night?"

Harper let out an angry scoff. "What did *I* do? Nothing!"

"You just said—"

"I went out with Alex. Nothing happened. We got a drink at Wings and I went home."

"Is Alex—"

"Yes, the guy from Buckerfield's. And he's as sexy and charming as I knew he would be, but I couldn't go through with it because Evan texted me halfway through, saying the neighbour came by looking for an air mattress. I panicked and went home." Harper glared at Jodi. "Couldn't have texted me first, huh?"

"Excuse me? You used me as an alibi—why didn't you text *me*?"

"Because I knew you'd talk me out of going! The one time I actually *needed* you to stay home and not talk to anyone, and you go over and have a chat with my husband? By the way, you're going by a new name. He asked who the friend was, and I had to think of one fast."

"What name?"

Harper sighed. "Vicki."

The way Jodi's stomach lurched made her actually fear throwing up. "You didn't."

"It's just when we're around Evan."

"You can't call me Vicki."

"Don't worry, it'll just be until he forgets. Which he will."

The way Harper waved it off. It was always just a weird story for her, Jodi knew. Even with the time Harper had knocked on the door during a screaming match. The way Harper tells it, she'd stepped between the two women, hand out to each, and comforted Jodi later with a hand stroking her hair. In reality, Harper had been there to say she could hear the shouts from her yard. She'd been slightly tipsy at the time, which could explain her less than accurate recollection.

Jodi tried to calm her breathing. "Why do you need to keep up the charade? Doesn't Evan know what you did?"

"No. I told him a guy *flirted* with me. I said you and I went to a restaurant, and some hot guy asked for my number."

"Why would you—"

"Because!" Harper let out another frustrated groan, then gestured harshly to herself. "Evan doesn't know what he's got. He wasn't even bothered—I have to scream at him to *get* bothered. And why in the hell did you need that mattress in the first place? If there was ever a time we needed it, it was last night. I wouldn't have gotten so pissed if I knew I'd have to sleep next to the guy!" Harper flicked a hand at the house, which they were approaching. Jodi hadn't realized they'd circled the neighbourhood already, and hoped Mr. Doucette wasn't peeking through the blinds.

"I...I went hiking."

"Bullshit."

"I did."

"You did not. That was an excuse you gave your mother to get out of Zumba."

Jodi opened her mouth to argue, then stopped herself. What good would it do? Jodi would prefer forgetting the trip altogether now. "You should tell Evan how you're feeling. He can't change if he doesn't know what's going on."

"Weren't you listening? I've screamed at him what I'm feeling. He doesn't get it."

"Then get a divorce."

Harper stopped walking, turning to glare at Jodi full on. "It's not that simple." She kept her voice low—they were right in front of Harper's house.

"I didn't say it was—"

"You did! You made it sound like I can just waltz inside and break up. Not all of us are lucky enough to have such a clear-cut end."

Jodi stared at her friend. "Excuse me?"

Guilt crossed Harper's face. "I didn't mean to word it like that...it's just, you know..."

"What?"

Harper was obviously struggling to find the words.

"Do you know how much I wish I had a normal break-up?" Jodi's hands were balled at her sides. "How much I wish my only issue was that Vicki didn't appreciate me?"

"All I'm saying is, well, from your perspective, the break-up was an easy choice."

"My breakup was decided by the fucking *internet!*" Jodi's voice rose on the last word. "Is that what you'd rather have? A public hearing? Because we all know how kindly the internet takes to cheaters."

"I didn't cheat—"

"Because you got scared and ran."

"I can't believe you're judging me. You."

"What's that supposed to mean?"

Harper pressed her lips together, like words were fighting to escape her mouth. Her eyes shone.

"What, Harper?"

"I just think you should be more supportive, that's all. Because I was the only one who didn't leave after Vicki posted that video."

Jodi knew she had a point, but still hated that Harper used it as a trump card. "That's because you know the truth. You lived next to me. You know how things were."

"We all make mistakes. That's what I'm saying."

"Yes, we do, but..." Jodi stared at her. "You don't believe I was actually like that. Do you?"

"I've moved on, Jodi. All I'm asking is that you be a little more understanding. I'm not pointing fingers."

"You..." Jodi faltered as it dawned on her. "You don't believe me. Which means you never believed me. You think I abused Vicki."

Harper looked uncomfortable. "I think things got heated—"

"I explained so many times. You nodded like you understood, Harper, I *told* you about how she would rile me up, how she'd set up the cameras...and you still don't believe me."

The two friends stood there, face to face, as the wind blew around them. Harper lifted her hands, a lost look on her face. "I'm willing to look *past* it, Jodi. That's better than just believing everything from your perspective. It means that I'm accepting you for who you are, no matter—"

"No." Jodi shook her head hard, backing away farther now. She yanked her phone out of her pocket and brandished it harshly. "No, this isn't me. It's not. And you've been the only person who connected who I know I am to reality, but if you never did, then..." *Then what?*

Before Jodi could formulate her next scattered thought, a sound cut the air. A ragged, unearthly screech.

Harper jumped and put hands over her ears, looking terrified. "What the hell is that?"

Jodi's heart pounded. "It's an animal. In pain." Jodi did a slow turn, trying to locate it. When the sound came again, Jodi pinpointed it at Harper's.

The two women ran back to the house, the noise growing louder. It was in the yard they found the source. It was a cat, writhing on the ground.

Things got worse once Jodi understood two things. One, that the cat's leg was clamped in the jaws of a mole trap, which had been dug out—but not disarmed. The second was that the cat was—

"Mini Wheats." Jodi fell to her knees. "Oh, no—"

"How did it get trapped?" Harper's voice was horror stricken. "Was it digging?"

"The trap was pulled out of the ground—"

A door crashed open, and Evan's voice cut Jodi off. "What the hell is going on?"

"Why is the trap out of the ground, Evan?" Harper rounded on her husband. "I didn't take it out."

"Is that a *cat?*" Evan gripped his hair. "Oh God, what the hell—"

"Why was the trap out?"

"I—I—" Evan's hands fell. "I was hurt—all you ever talked about was these frigging traps, I don't know, I wasn't thinking, it was a fit of passion—"

"So you just yanked them out of the ground and left them here?"

"I didn't know they could be set off above ground, I thought it needed the pressure of the dirt—"

Jodi was trying, in vain, to understand how the trap worked. It looked like a pair of claws. "Can someone please help me undo this?"

Harper's face was pallid. "I can't do it."

Evan knelt, but immediately stood back up. "I don't know how it works—I don't want to hurt it even more." His voice was wobbling.

Mini Wheats' eyes were huge, her ears flat to her head. The moment Jodi touched the trap, Mini Wheats hissed and scrambled to get away. Jodi could feel tears hot on her cheeks now—every second was torture for the cat, but Jodi was too scared to do anything.

What would Rae do?

Rae would be calm, for one. They might take the trap off, or they might give some reason why it wasn't a good idea. The trap could be the only thing keeping Mini Wheats from bleeding out. Either way, the necessary action was clear.

"I need to get her to an emergency vet." Jodi yanked her mackinaw off and, wincing, managed to wrap it around the cat and the trap and pick both off the ground.

"Evan will drive you." Harper gave a filthy look at her husband, then whirled, and headed back to the house.

Chapter 10

The waiting room was tiny. Lucky for Jodi, they were the only ones there—the vet had taken Mini Wheats immediately into the back.

Jodi went to sit down next to Evan. Only at that moment did she realize her hands were shaking.

"We can probably go now." Evan gestured to the closed examination room door. "They'll take care of her."

"I'm not leaving Mini Wheats here alone."

"Mini Wheats?" Evan blinked. "Same name as Harper's friend Jodi's cat. Is it popular for cats?"

Anger flashed through Jodi. She didn't owe Harper anything—but it didn't mean she wanted to be a catalyst in a fight. No explanation that made sense came to her, however, and she'd just made the decision to stay silent when the receptionist called out, "It's Jodi with an *i*, not *y*, correct?"

Jodi winced. "Yep, that's right."

Evan looked forward. Jodi could see the wheels turning. His mouth pressed in a hard line, and his eyes were suddenly shining.

Jodi studied her hands. There was a smear of dried blood on one; she wiped it on her overalls. "You don't have to stay."

"Yeah, I think I'm gonna go." He stood and pulled on his jacket, then shook his head, clearly fighting to stay composed. "You'd think my wife would've planned an affair better."

"I'm sorry." It was all Jodi could say.

"I can't believe she'd use you as an excuse, but not even tell you." He tried a cynical laugh that was ruined by it breaking in the middle. "I'm usually the one making the dumb decisions."

"And yet it worked." Jodi was still trying to get the blood off her hands. She'd have to wash them properly, but she wasn't sure if the vet had a public bathroom. "Ironically, Evan, the fact that you never remember the name of your wife's friend is my favourite thing about you. I wish everyone would forget."

Evan was frozen for a second, likely trying to think of a retort, but unable. The door closed hard behind him, tinkling a bell at the top.

It was barely the afternoon, and Jodi was more exhausted than she'd been in a long time. She might've even dropped off for a few minutes because she jolted awake when the vet called her name.

Disoriented, she stood and wobbled over to the counter. "How is she?"

The vet, a short, severe woman with cropped blue hair, went into detail with zero preamble, which Jodi appreciated. "Your girl's leg was broken by the trap. With a fracture this severe, and with the lack of blood flow to the limb before the trap was removed, the best course of action would be to amputate."

"She'd lose her leg?" Jodi asked stupidly.

"It sounds horrible, and it is, but in truth a cat can adjust and thrive with just three. It would be better than trying in vain to save a leg that may cause her pain the rest of her life."

A lump was in Jodi's throat. "Could...could I have helped? If I took the trap off sooner?" She didn't want to cry in front of the stern-looking vet, but it might happen.

The vet softened. "You didn't do anything wrong. She needed to be sedated before the trap was removed—more damage was very possible if you attempted to take it off yourself. It could've torn the leg more, or snapped closed in a different spot, or she could've run off."

Jodi nodded, willing the tears not to fall.

"We're going to prep for surgery immediately. You said on your intake form that the cat was a *stray, kind of*—does this mean you're relinquishing the cat to a shelter? There isn't any microchip or tattoo, so that's where she'd go."

Jodi knew what the vet was asking. This surgery was going to cost money—a lot of money. If Jodi didn't want to pay, she had to accept the fact that Mini Wheats would go to a shelter, where many adoptable cats already waited for homes. Where nearly half—the less cute half, the less-hair half, the less-than-four-leg half—were eventually euthanized.

"If I kept her, how much…" Jodi cleared her throat, which was dry, "how much is this going to cost?"

The vet regarded her for several moments. Then she said a number that made Jodi's ears ring.

But images kept playing in Jodi's head. Mini Wheats bumping her ragged little head against Jodi's side. Jamming her face against Jodi's fingernails. Sitting happily under the lampshade. Splayed across Jodi's lap, purring and heavy, like she knew Jodi needed that real thing grounding her to reality.

Jodi swallowed. "Is there a payment plan?"

There was sympathy in the vet's expression as she gave instruction to the receptionist. After signing some forms, Jodi returned to her chair, drained physically and financially.

Heart heavy with shame, she pulled out her phone and dialed a number. It went to voicemail. "Hi, Mum…" She closed her eyes tight.

* * *

Jodi slumped in the chair, staring at the fibreboard ceiling. Her mind was on herself, three years ago. She made good money working for a marketing company. She had friends from university. Her father was alive, which meant she had a solid safety net of two parents, no matter how formal and tense. Her self-image was solid. She knew who she was.

There was little left of that person now. Tiny bits were chipped off with each loss. Her father took one. The boss who had let her go for "budgetary reasons," but couldn't hide the distrust in his eyes put there via his more internet-savvy employees, took another. Each friend who met Jodi's messages with a perfunctory one-word response or emoji or—sometimes—with nothing at all, took bits of their own.

It was partly Jodi's fault. She didn't fight hard enough. At the time, she thought the truth was enough. Unfortunately, the truth, in this case, needed to be screamed. It needed her to follow behind and repeat the facts until one sounded believable enough for a person to turn back. She was saying the words so often spoken by the deplorables, the world simply didn't have the patience to listen.

It isn't what it looks like. It wasn't my fault. She forced me.

It was getting to the point where Jodi didn't believe herself.

Desperate for a distraction, Jodi scrolled through her phone apps aimlessly. At times like this she wished she engaged in social media still—she needed the mindlessness of escaping into the chaos.

After clearing some storage and changing her phone's theme from green to darker green, Jodi was back to being in her brain, which wasn't ideal. After a moment's contemplation, she realized there was one more thing she could do. Although it wasn't going to steer her from bad thoughts, it would at least be somewhat productive. Even if it led nowhere.

After navigating to her cloud storage, she scrolled until she found the newest folder. *STRANGE SD CARD*. After putting in her wireless headphones, she tapped the first video and clicked the volume up.

The video started out focused on a sizzling steak in a pan, and Jodi let out a breath of relief. Dinnertime. Not early in the trip, when Grant was setting up, or driving. And it wasn't another camper's card altogether.

It wasn't terribly interesting. Without her editing program Jodi didn't have a precise way of scrubbing through silence, and she didn't want to miss anything, so she settled for guessing where his pauses ended and backtracking when she went too far forward. His attitude was normal and peppy, though he spent some time ranting about the high-tech RVs that occupied a few camp spots for the weekend. ("It's not real camping—those rich phonies might as well build a house while they're at it.") He then gave a long speech about Gandhi while he ate.

Jodi found herself zoning out as Grant went on. She was so tired, his voice was hypnotic, and he was now talking about a sitcom he hated. Jodi slapped her cheeks to wake up, eliciting a concerned glance from the receptionist. Jodi gave a smile to assure she wasn't going mental and continued on to the next video.

The afternoon waned as Jodi went through two and a half hours of footage. Grant ate, then cleaned up his food waste. With relief, Jodi watched as he walked to his truck with the bag, leaving nothing for bears to smell.

Then, Grant was swearing under his breath. He put down the bag next to the truck, and the camera was flicking around as he turned his head in every direction.

Jodi sat up in her chair, staring at the phone. Her heart hammered.

Grant returned to the tent, which he promptly tore apart, cursing up a storm. "I know they were in my pocket." Grant's hands dug in the bedding, then threw it all aside, exposing the cot. "Must've fallen out when I went swimming. That's not it, Danny Dewitt."

His keys.
He lost his keys.

The revelation hit Jodi like a truck. If he never found the keys, Grant couldn't go home that night, even if he wanted to.

After an unsuccessful search, Grant remade his bed, temper high. The video cut off suddenly, meaning his battery wore down. Likely he'd forgotten the camera was on.

Jodi took a minute to absorb this new information. Grant had lost his keys. It was an entirely logical and non-deadly reason his truck sat abandoned in the campsite. With no cellphone signal, he had no way to contact a locksmith or BCAA.

Her underarms were sweaty as she clicked the next video.

The screen was entirely dark, though there was a lot of commotion. Grant's voice was low, but no less hot-tempered. "Have to move this gotdamn tent. Can't stand the smell. Some rich RV asshole must've leaked all over this site."

There wasn't a lot of proper footage—Grant must've realized that there wasn't enough light to film and was likely too frustrated to bother. But there was an update once the tent was set up, with him confirming that, upon many sniffs of the ground, this site was gasoline-free.

The next video started with a head-cam shot of eggs bubbling in a pan. "Morning, all. Sorry for the Grant Rant last night.

Trademark. I went for a dip this morning in freezing cold waters, and still couldn't find my keys. If I had cell signal, I'd call my kid for a ride. But then, would probably get some excuse or another. Mentioned something about a party this weekend. Who knows what kids are doing these days. Can't count on them."

Jodi winced, imagining Rae watching this.

The next video started with a shot of Grant's feet walking on gravel, and Jodi's heartrate increased. She knew the card ended up back at the camp, but there needed to be something. Some clue about why he disappeared.

The camera went up, and there was a big, fancy RV. Outside, a child sat in the dirt, playing on a phone.

"Hey, buddy." Grant's hand waved. "Listen, I need to contact someone for help. I see you've got a cool-looking satellite on top of that RV. You mind if I use your phone?"

The kid's expression was wary. "I don't think I'm allowed."

"All right, how about this—you give me your Wi-Fi password. I think that's a pretty fair compromise. You guys are taking up all the signal, you should share."

The kid was nervous, but Grant's needling was effective. "I think the password is Summerfamily, with a capital S."

"Good boy." Grant waved, then circled the RV, and sat down on a tree stump. His phone appeared, and after a few attempts managed to connect to the RV's Wi-Fi. Jodi watched as Grant navigated to a messaging app and sent texts to a few people—none of whom were Rae.

The video ended before any return messages. It was the last video.

Jodi stared at the black screen of her phone, lost in thought. Though there wasn't definitive proof, it was now likely that Grant had gotten a ride off the campsite. The search parameter was no longer limited to how far he'd gotten on foot.

All she wanted was to call Rae and ask if they'd managed to watch the videos, but the last interaction burned in her mind. Before her fight with Harper, Jodi had harboured a scrap of hope that, after a while, she might be able to convince Rae to see her side. Now...now she wondered if it was worth trying. If two years didn't work on her best friend, then there wasn't much hope convincing anyone.

Jodi was yanked from her brain by the reappearance of the vet, who was in good spirits. The surgery went well, and Mini Wheats—now Minier Wheats, one leg less—was zonked out and resting. Jodi was allowed to visit and stroked her head with a finger through the cage.

"She's not out of the woods yet. There was a lot of blood loss. I'll give you a call tomorrow, no matter what."

Jodi nodded, keeping her eyes on her cat. "I'll get you some better food," she whispered.

"I'm glad this one has you." The vet's voice was soft as she handed Jodi back her mackinaw, which was stained with dried blood. "Most aren't this lucky."

* * *

After a too-expensive Uber home, Jodi sat at her computer, exhausted. All she wanted to do was go to bed and forget the day, but knew something else needed to be done for her conscience to be clear. So she booted up her computer and loaded the final video into her editing program.

After scrubbing to the very end, she zoomed in on the phone screen and did what she could to enhance the shot in her photo editing program. Movies and TV set unrealistic standards on how much someone could clear up a blurry image, but she could help somewhat. She wrote down the names—there were only first names, no last—of the people Grant messaged, and what she could discern from their tiny profile pictures. Then she constructed a carefully worded, rigidly formal text and sent it, along with the screenshots and an invoice—a fair one, which subtracted the cost of a groom—to the person whose arms she'd slept in the night before.

There. Jodi dropped her phone on the desk. She was done.

She had done what Rae had wanted from her. She had used what skills and resources she had to help them. Whether the two of them were even, she didn't know. But she did know that Rae didn't need her anymore.

It should have been freeing. Rae had complicated Jodi's life in the short time they were there. But Jodi couldn't kid herself. Despite everything, Rae's existence made her happier. It made her see herself again. Just a glimpse of the way she saw herself before. Briefly, Rae had held a rosy mirror, before bringing it down hard on a knee.

Jodi chewed on her lip, then stood and walked into her bathroom. She forced herself to stare in the mirror, which wasn't something she did often. Not full on. Not more than a glance—she'd gotten proficient at applying mascara without looking.

Her face was so much hollower. Years ago, she'd have called it round, with a rosy tint to her cheeks and chin and forehead. Now, her cheeks pushed in, and the circles under her eyes overwhelmed any pinkness. Unable to look any longer, Jodi reached forward and pulled open the mirror cabinet, revealing the many piles of unopened floss packages.

Despite Vicki's channel using fake names, and despite Jodi's best attempts at scrubbing the internet free of her presence, some sleuths had found Jodi's personal information. The packages had been a not-so-subtle act of revenge on the viewers' part. Jodi didn't look too far into it, but she had a pretty good guess what it meant. *Give enough rope...*

Slowly, she gathered the floss packages, then dumped them onto her bed. After arranging them neatly, she took a photo, then posted it online for ten dollars.

If life tells you to kill yourself, use it to help pay a vet bill.

Jodi walked through her suite, photographing and posting anything she could spare. It was therapeutic. *The vase she made? Gone. The lamp we thrifted? Sayonara.* It didn't matter if they failed to sell—just the fact that Jodi was telling the world to take them away was freeing.

There was a hard knock on her front door. Jodi stepped over the piles of stuff she was photographing and ran to get it. It was Harper, looking even worse for wear than before.

The two stared at each other. Harper's eyes were flicking around, as though it were painful to meet Jodi's.

Harper was the first to speak. "Well? What happened with the cat?"

"They amputated the leg."

Harper wrinkled her nose briefly, looking sick. "I feel awful. It shouldn't have happened."

"No, it shouldn't have."

"Evan's an idiot, he…" Harper swallowed, and tears welled in her eyes. "Well, he's not even thinking about the cat thing right now. He thinks I cheated, which isn't even true."

She backed up and sat on the cement stairs, head in hands. Jodi said nothing.

Harper's mouth twisted, and she continued as though Jodi accused her: "Jodi, I did *nothing*. We had one drink. I probably wouldn't have gone through with it, Jesus. I just wanted a taste. That's all. And now Evan's talking about divorce." Harper's eyes went everywhere but Jodi. "You could have at least tried to cover for me. You could have been Vicki for one hour."

That sentence was like a stab. "I wasn't putting a fake name on paperwork, Harper—and the receptionist called it out, not me. If I'm paying a grand in vet bills, I've got to put my own name down, haven't I?"

Harper finally looked at Jodi, confused. "Vet bill? Girl, you don't have to pay for a stray."

"She's not a stray. She's mine."

Harper stared at her. "You can't keep that cat."

"Yes, I can."

"You're not even allowed a cat in this suite."

"Well, I probably won't be staying in this place for long—"

"Jodi, we're not paying any of it. We can't afford it, especially if we've got counselling or legal fees in the future."

Jodi knew this was coming. Somehow, she knew. And yet, she couldn't help it. "That trap was Evan's fault."

"It was our property. The cat was trespassing. And if it was your cat, then you accept the risk of it being hurt if you let it outside. That's all part of having a cat."

This conversation was twisting the knife. Jodi knew Harper was technically correct. Yet, she couldn't help the anger roiling in her as she stared at her only friend. "Blame just rolls off you, doesn't it? Sticks to me, though."

Harper leapt to her feet, eyes on fire. "Oh yeah, my life is great. Fabulous. I've slaved ten years as the better person in a relationship, and I'm the one getting kicked out of it. I'll be remembered as the bad guy, Jodi. For nothing. For a bad beer at a greasy restaurant. And now you're blaming me for the trap being out, which is something Evan did to *spite* me. To sabotage the one thing keeping me sane. The one thing I was trying to fix. He'll get that lawn, you know, if we divorce. He'll get the house, and the lawn will go to shit, and he'll be like 'how did that happen, it happened out of nowhere, wasn't my fault, I didn't do anything,' just like he always fucking does." There were tears in her eyes, running down her face, and she was jabbing her finger in Jodi's direction like a curse. "And then you get to run around with weird, gorgeous strangers at thirty fucking two, and you complain about your free life with your stay-at-home job and man-free basement suite, and you've already gone through the bad bit after a breakup. And you couldn't just go by Vicki for a single godforsaken hour."

A lump was in Jodi's throat, but she forced herself to speak. "I already set up a financing plan with the vet. I assumed you wouldn't pay, so don't worry about it."

Harper's jaw twitched, and she shook her head hard. "Don't blame me for a decision you made."

"Then don't you do the same."

"I wasn't going to cheat!" Harper whirled and hurried up the stairs.

Jodi sped after her, rocks biting into her bare feet on the cold cement. "Yeah, that's what you said. Isn't it frustrating when your friend doesn't believe you, no matter how many times you say it?"

Harper threw Jodi a filthy look over her shoulder, but it was mixed with hurt, and she nearly bumped into a man heading in Jodi's direction. He wore a dusty jumpsuit, with a respirator hanging around his neck. "Sorry." He watched Harper continue on towards her house, then faced Jodi, who was doing her best to calm her shuddering breaths. "I'm looking for Jodi?"

Jodi balanced on one foot and flicked away a rock embedded in her heel. "Yes, that's me."

"Hi there. I'm here to patch a hole." He gestured to the van sitting in the driveway, with *Patch Happy Solutions* decaled on the side.

Jodi took another steadying breath. Mr. Doucette had not told her—he'd assumed she was always home, which before this week was entirely true.

Jodi led the man to her workstation, to the hole behind the rippling plastic. The man got to work, unloading his tools. "Don't worry, I'll get this ugly thing all patched for you." His eyes strayed to her computer. "That's a nice computer. Boyfriend's?"

"Mine."

"Dang, took a guess. I don't usually see computers like that in a girl's place, that's really cool. Do you play games on it?"

Jodi's fight with Harper was pounding in her head; the small talk from the drywaller was more than she could bear. "No, sorry. Listen, I'm heading out—will you be fine working without me here?"

Surprise passed over the man's face. "Oh, yeah, that's totally cool—"

"Great. Uh, good luck. Lychee drinks are in the fridge." Jodi slipped on her shoes, found a cardigan to wear—her mackinaw was too blood-covered—and left as fast as possible.

In her car, Jodi stared forward, hands on the wheel. For a moment she imagined pulling onto the freeway and driving east. How far could she get on the gas she had? How far could she get with her credit card and whatever toonies she had left?

It was just a daydream, she knew. The truth was, she couldn't escape. Those millions of views didn't stop at the borders of her town. It didn't even stop at the borders of her country. She could cross an ocean and still have to present her defence on every date and carry worry and uncertainty into every job. Harper was right before. There was no running. Today, that thought carried less misery than usual.

Running was futile, which meant she could rest.

Eventually the notoriety would fade. The video of Jodi Marples laying an angry hand on her cowering girlfriend would be buried under the glut of horrors on the internet, and she would resurface only occasionally on "disturbing media" compilation videos and listicles.

Despite Jodi's bone-deep exhaustion, the day's events had done something peculiar. They had lifted a weight she hadn't even known was burdening her. Seeing the truth in both Harper and Rae's expressions meant it was over. Her worst fears had come to pass. As of this moment, they had reacted to the worst of her with the worst of reactions.

And yet, she was still here.

Jodi gazed through her sunroof. "I'm still here, Vicki. I'm not sure if that makes you happy or not, but it's the truth. And I'm not going anywhere."

The first raindrops of the day plunked down on the sunroof. Jodi smiled weakly, then yanked her keys out of the ignition and opened her door to get out. It was time she got her free flight of beer.

The distance to the brewery was short, but two minutes in her hair was soaked and her cardigan was heavy with rain. She normally disliked walking, especially in the rain, but today she didn't mind. Inside her was the painful freedom of an animal chewing itself out of a trap—it was done, and things were lost, but life goes on. She had to accept it all—even if it meant accepting a past self she didn't recognize.

As she crossed the parking lot, her eye caught the silver Hyundai parked near the door of the brewery, and she stopped short. It took several long seconds of staring before she shook her head and continued to the door. *So many people have silver Hyundais.*

And yet, when she entered the brewery, her eyes locked immediately onto Rae, sitting alone at the bar.

For a breath she froze in the doorway, debating turning around and heading back to her car. But then Rae twisted to stretch their back and caught sight of Jodi.

The moment sat heavy on both of them. Rae stayed mid-back-crack, eyes startled. Jodi wondered if turning around and leaving would make a point, or if it would make her a coward.

She didn't get to make the choice, because an old woman tottered up behind her with a wide walker that made no room for exiting smoothly. So Jodi stepped into the brewery and, figuring things couldn't get worse, walked up to Rae. "Is this seat taken?"

Rae shook their head.

Jodi hopped up on the stool and pulled her wet cardigan off. "I swear I wasn't stalking you. Just needed a beer."

Rae gestured to their plate. "You mentioned they had good grilled cheese."

Jodi recalled their first conversation. "That's right, I did. Same conversation you refused to share a free flight with me." She pulled out the free flight card and waved it. "Glad I didn't, in hindsight."

A server came over, and Jodi ordered a mix of craft beers before turning back to Rae. "So? Did you find a place to watch the videos?"

"I did. And I got your texts." Rae toyed with one half of the grilled cheese. "It's a good thing you can zoom in properly, because I thought that one profile picture of a motorbike was a cow. Was calling local dairy farms, asking if anyone picked up some guy from a campsite on their milk truck."

"So you don't recognize the names?"

"Nope." Rae took a drink of beer. "My dad's life is rich with weird people I have never met. Probably people he knew from a local poetry reading, or a highland bagpipe concert." Rae tapped their phone, which was next to the plate. "You'd think from his videos that he was some recluse, but the truth is, he has a better social life than I do."

"Could've fooled me."

"Never believe what you see online, I guess." Rae continued staring at the grilled cheese. "Hearing what my dad said about me hurt."

"Bet it did."

"Whether he actually forgot about my grand opening party or was just making things up for the camera, I don't know. But watchers would have assumed I was a loser, all because his was the story that made it online." Rae sighed, tapping absently on their phone, then focused on Jodi. "I reacted on impulse and shock. No matter what, you should have the chance to tell your side of the story. So..." Rae put down their phone and waved a hand.

Jodi fiddled with the cuticle on her thumb. Having the chance to speak damn near tied her vocal cords. She cleared her throat and ran desperately in her head through ways to start this. Wondered which was the best path that showed her side in the most even light. "How many videos have you watched?"

"A lot. Whatever I could find that involved you."

Jodi winced, then took a moment to down one of her little glasses of beer. Finally, she began. "Vicki was an amazing woman."

Rae leaned back in the chair, eyes on Jodi.

"She drew eyes in a room. She was in my marketing class at university, and it was like she was the personification of it. Gorgeous, confident, funny, generous. She was already a decently popular influencer when I met her, and it was obvious why. You just wanted to be near her. She was this whirlpool, pulling us all in. We all wanted to be her friend. She was fantastic at making friends.

"She was also an abuser."

The words were hard to say, even now. They felt like someone else's words, and she felt like a thief for using them. Had to remind herself that she wasn't.

"It started slow, as I've read it often does. The honeymoon period was bliss—I was so stunned to be by her side, I wouldn't have noticed red flags if they were waved in my face. Now, I can remember things, even at the beginning. Taking my phone, accusing me of hiding things if I didn't let her look through it, that kind of thing.

"As it progressed, I never said anything to anyone. I was deeply in love, and anything physical was so infrequent that I could justify it. She played the size card a lot—she was taller, but lighter, daintier. She could hit me because she weighed less. *That was so baby,* she'd say after she'd calmed down, even though it sure didn't feel baby. The bruises and cuts from her little nail jewels didn't feel baby. The hole she'd elbowed in the wall that I cut around in a bad attempt to disguise it from my landlord didn't feel baby. But everything else about her was out of my league. I didn't want to lose her humour, her beauty, her charm—all of it—because of a few bad fights.

"It was also hard because Vicki had this way of twisting the fight until I was the only one apologizing. I wasn't always in the right, either—I know that—but fights with her were in a parallel universe. I never shouted before Vicki. I hate being rude, and I hate confrontation, but here I was, screaming at this person I loved. It was unbelievable. A tiny ripple of disagreement would build until she'd be sending tidal waves of accusations and misunderstandings and insults. For me, it was like bellowing at a waterfall—my voice was lost in the tumult, but I still kept trying. I hated myself with her. I never hated myself more than I did at that point. Or since." Jodi paused. This was the point at which people with expressive faces would show their skepticism. A mini eyeroll, or furtive glances that said *yeah, yeah. The old "she got me angry" excuse.*

Rae did not have an expressive face; their expression was as neutral as it was when she started. "Did you know she was filming?"

"Sometimes." Jodi took a sip of beer to lubricate her dry mouth. "Not often. Her phone and camera were always set up on tripods, so she would sometimes just hit record mid-fight. I didn't know about the videos—most of them—until way later. I didn't go on the app, and she was always showing me the videos she posted. I didn't know there were more she wasn't showing me."

"Have you watched them?"

"Not all. It hurts. All I know is that those videos are edited to some degree. She always did her own editing, even though I offered to help. I don't remember the details of our fights, but I'm sure they didn't go like that." Jodi paused, staring at her beer. "I'm almost sure. That's the thing about the world screaming that your memory is wrong—you start believing it after a while.

"The problem was that she was actually quite good at editing, even with just a phone app. It looked and sounded so seamless and believable. It was so easy to fall into the paranoia that it was me, all along. That there was no dramatic editing after all—I was just an abuser who forgot. All I could do was remind myself of the differences."

"What do you mean? The differences?"

"Between her old and new videos. All the older ones, where I was normal and we just did happy couple things—they were edited differently. Back when I was still able to look at the videos," Jodi held up fingers, "I did math to keep me sane. Old videos: average of ten seconds between cuts. New videos: average of three. Old videos: eighty percent of the time, you can see my mouth moving. New videos: mouth visible only forty percent of the time. Things like that. It was all I had, these differences. It was the only thing I could clutch onto—those workarounds that meant it was possible those videos weren't showing the real me. But I can't deny that some of the videos were more real than others.

"The parts with me being physical? They're real. I am a person who got violent, who put hands on her partner. I can never take back that fact. But, if you'll give me a moment, I can explain how I got there."

Rae may have indicated for her to go ahead, but Jodi was already talking. At this point, it didn't matter if Rae got up and left; Jodi needed to tell this part of the story, with every dirty detail, even if it was only heard by the wood of the bar and the fruit fly currently dying in her beer glass. "There was one video involving floss. It's why I keep getting floss packets mailed to me by ironic viewers who want me to hang myself with it—bad omen, like I said. I think the video's notoriety was because it's the first physical video—I throw the floss packet at the wall and yell something about the floss being wrong. I'm pretty sure Vicki's crying was added later, but I definitely did scream and throw the packet. What you don't see is the pain I'm in, and you also can't see the time—if a clock was in the shot, you'd see it's about three thirty in the morning. She must've been careful not to get clocks in frame.

"A week previous, I had gotten some dental work done, and one area wasn't healing right. It was agony to chew on, and it was so sensitive that flossing was like scraping the tooth with a rasp. But having food in there hurt worse, so I had to floss anyway. I found that the pain was worse when I used this certain kind of floss that she'd bought—it was abrasive, and it frayed easily. There was another kind that didn't hurt as bad. It was softer, flatter, and smoother, and it made the pain bearable.

"She always insisted on getting the groceries. It was her thing, and she would get offended if I went. But for some reason, she kept getting me the wrong floss. And even though it hurt, I had to use it until the next grocery day, only for her to get the wrong kind again. After the third time, I asked if she was doing it on purpose. It was the wrong thing to say.

"I'd never seen her so angry. She got cruel, calling me weak, screaming at me for distrusting her, for trying to make her feel stupid. But I was fed up and in pain and tired from a few bad nights of sleep—I just kept asking how she continued getting the wrong kind, because I'd sent her a picture, and the two brands couldn't look more different. All she said was that I was ungrateful, I was making up the pain. And she wouldn't stop— the fight lasted hours. Fifteen minutes in I wanted to end the argument. I apologized, but she wouldn't let it go. I went to bed, but she kept waking me up to continue the fight, repeating the same accusations again and again. That clip of me—I was sleep deprived, my tooth was in pain, and she'd just woken me for the tenth time by throwing the packet hard at my neck."

Jodi paused, trying to judge Rae's expression. It was impassive, so she just kept going.

"The time I hit her..." Jodi swallowed. She hated this story, but knew it was her duty to tell it. "My cousin needed to rehome her cat, Jetson. Her newborn daughter was allergic, so I offered to cat-sit until she found him a home. Secretly, I wanted to keep the cat—he was such a good boy, a real cuddler. I knew Vicki didn't really like animals, but she agreed to keep Jetson for a week or so, and I loved her for it. I figured he'd grow on her. He was that kind of cat.

"I think a secret part of me saw him as a peacemaker. It was hard to imagine such anger and resentment and fear existing in his proximity—he would suck up the negative energy like a big, floppy, orange mop. But I saw, straight off, that Vicki wasn't good with him. She complained about his hair and his smell whenever he was near her.

She would kind of kick him to get him to move—that was a big argument. I think part of it got in a video. Still, I held out hope that she'd warm to him.

"That is, until one day I got home from work and she...she was holding him. For a second, I was happy that they were getting along. But then she looked at me, smiled, and drop kicked him, hard, against a wall."

Rae's eyebrows shot up. "She *what?*"

"That's when I ran at her. I was going to go to Jetson, but I was scared of what I might see. There was no movement where he'd landed, and there was blood on the wall.

"Partly, I was thinking that Vicki was in a psychotic episode. I knew she had anger issues, but I didn't think she was sadistic. I never thought she enjoyed, you know...hitting. This was a level above, and I wanted to snap her out of whatever psychosis she was in. But part of it was also rage. It was rage for Jetson, and for me." Jodi pressed the heels of her hands to her eyes. "I slapped her across the face, then grabbed her arms and shook her. And...and..." Jodi drew a shuddering breath. "Vicki just slid out of my hands to the floor, weeping, and that was when Jetson came trotting out of the kitchen, meowing for food. The thing she'd kicked was a stuffed orange cat plushie she'd bought at a thrift store. Later, I found out she'd filled it with rice and red Jello, just to give the prank realism. That's what she called it, later. A prank. Which was why she filmed it. The kick never made the cut, though."

The two of them sat in silence for a moment. Jodi drank another of her little cups—the beer was tart and tasted of raspberry. Rae, absently, picked up one of Jodi's beers as well and downed it. "I assume the relationship ended there."

Jodi shook her head.

"You're kidding."

"I wanted to. But she convinced me to try mending things. I was willing to do anything she asked at that point, even if it felt wrong." Jodi wiped a line through the condensation on one of her beer glasses. "It wasn't long after when I got a bunch of hateful messages on an old account of mine, referencing Vicki. I logged in and made a new account—she'd blocked mine—and finally saw the videos she never told me about. I can't describe that feeling. Knowing that she'd kept moments she'd sworn to have deleted. Seeing an exaggerated form of my worst self condensed into bite-sized segments. Knowing that the world had seen them, shared them, made comments and video responses to them.

"I confronted her about it. I forced myself to stay calm, no matter what she did, now that I knew she recorded all our fights. Stupidly, I didn't think to record this conversation myself. It probably wouldn't have revealed much, though. Like with the floss thing, she can't really be convinced she did something wrong. She refused to admit the videos were heavily edited—she just kept insisting I remembered things wrong, that she barely did anything but cut out pauses, that she'd showed me every video before posting. I asked her to remove them, but she said they were already out there, and she couldn't just ruin her career like that.

"We broke up, but the damage was done. People I knew in real life came across those videos, and with Vicki sticking with her story, I didn't have a lot to stand on. Some people called the police, and I had to go in for questioning. It never went anywhere because Vicki refused to press charges, made up some story that got us both off the hook. I could have sued her for defamation, but it would've taken money, and I might've just lost—it was her word against mine in court, and she was so unbelievably charming. I lost my job, and a lot of my friends. In the beginning I assumed just telling them the truth was enough. It was only after when I realized they never believed me." She drank her last glass in one big gulp. "I was trying to convince them it was a motorbike, and everything about it looked like a cow. Can't really blame them. It's a convincing cow." The beer hit her suddenly, and she pressed a hand to her head. "Golly. I haven't drunk in a while."

"You want some of my sandwich?"

"Oh, well, if you're offering." Jodi reached over and took half of the sandwich, then bit into it ferociously. She was swallowing and taking another bite before noticing the look on Rae's face. "Please tell me you weren't joking. Do you want it back?"

"Absolutely not. I was just processing the speed at which you took it."

"Don't offer me food you're afraid to lose." The beer and nerves were making her giddy. It was impossible to look at Rae right now, so she focused on the chalkboard list of draft beers behind the bar. "So the question is this: do you believe me—a woman with zero evidence to back up her story—or do you believe what everyone does? The videos and statements of a dead woman?"

Rae's eyes went wide with disbelief. "Dead? She's *dead?*"

"Oh. Yes, she died. I should have told you that first." Jodi stared at a dollop of mustard on her thumb. "Car accident, two months after we broke up. You probably saw it in the news."

Rae shook their head minutely. "I barely look at the news."

"Really? Then why were you so damn smug about it when we met?" Jodi patted their hand, careful not to get mustard on it. "Sorry. You weren't smug. You were smug about my mug, though. You had a smug mug about my mug." Despite her brain urging her to stop, she found herself talking nonsense, afraid of any break in the conversation.

Because there was hope in there, too. Deep inside. Something about how Rae wasn't leaving, wasn't scoffing, as they had earlier—it gave her hope that, at the very least, they were seeing a small sliver of her side. It was all she needed—she didn't deserve to shrug all the guilt off her shoulders. Just a portion. Just enough to convince herself that, no matter the past, there was hope to lead a life as someone good.

Finally, Jodi chanced a look at Rae. Unfortunately, their gaze was fixated over her shoulder.

Before Jodi could turn, a voice rang out—"This place is a bitch to find, Rae. I missed the turn twice—who the hell designed the roads that way?"

Dread in her heart, Jodi focused on the bar, wishing she could blend right into it. Anything to avoid sliding off her seat and making an obvious escape. Because even though she'd only heard it twice, there was no mistaking Alpine's raspy, bright, excited voice.

"Talking up the ladies, My Treasure? Regaling them with stories about impacted anal glands?"

Knowing it would be worse if she avoided it, Jodi turned. Alpine's smile twitched as recognition glazed her face.

"We chanced upon each other here," Rae explained. "We've just been talking."

It took a few seconds for Alpine to recalibrate. "Ah." She returned her attention to Rae and held up a familiar baggie. "So you left this in my computer, genius."

"Sorry."

"No worries, because guess what." She slapped the SD card into Rae's hand. "I did some deducing, and I figured it out. Why would your dad leave most of his stuff behind? Logically?"

Rae shook their head, as though clearing it. "Well…because he couldn't carry it."

"Right. *Or.* The *vehicle* he was in couldn't carry it." Her eyes were wide, and she was nodding and grinning. Then she brought up her hands and mimicked revving. "Vroom vroom."

Realization dawned on Rae's face. "Motorbike."

Shock hit Jodi. *Alpine is right.* It made total sense, and she regretted not putting it together before. The image of Grant on the back of a motorbike, rattail blowing in the wind, seemed wild and completely plausible.

"Bingo." Alpine whipped out her phone. "We've just got to scour the internet and find this cow-shaped motorbike dude. He's got to be there—no one's anonymous anymore."

Alpine was deliberately keeping her eyes only on Rae. Jodi slid off her stool and, discreetly, pulled on her cardigan. She mouthed *I'm going* to Rae, who wasn't even paying attention—their eyes were locked on the middle distance, mind focused on this new possibility. Suddenly mortified, having realized she had crashed Alpine and Rae's meetup, Jodi scooted to the door.

It was still raining. Just as she stepped into the parking lot, she paused, chewing her lip hard.

She had found that SD card. She had found it after spending a night in a spider-infested tent. It didn't matter that it was awkward—that credit was Jodi's, not Alpine's.

The feeling rose, until she set her jaw and whirled to go back inside, only to come face-to-face with Alpine. The door closed behind her, and the two women stood in the rain together.

"What are you doing?" Alpine's tone was blunt.

Jodi swallowed. "I was leaving."

"You were coming back inside."

Jodi struggled to find words. "I wanted to ask if I could help, considering I know the footage pretty well. Plus, you know. I was the one who found it."

Alpine nodded slowly. "It's been, what, less than a week? Why are you so involved with Rae's life?"

Jodi stared at her. "I was helping—"

"Listen." Alpine brought up a hand. "Rae is my friend. And I'm not letting them get involved with someone like you."

"You don't know me."

"I don't need to."

"Those videos aren't the complete truth. I was the one getting hit."

The words came easier now. And yet, Alpine still scoffed. "Yeah, I remember a video Vicki put out about that. How you claim she abused you, but conveniently have zero evidence. You're just lucky you never went to jail."

Jodi's stomach fell. She hadn't seen that video. Jodi had never claimed abuse publicly, and had never even said the word to Vicki's face. It was always *got mad* or *freaked out*, forever walking on eggshells with the terminology. Yet Vicki foresaw Jodi's rebuttal, and had sown the seeds of doubt before Jodi had even opened her mouth.

Alpine lowered her voice. "And frankly, I wouldn't care if you're the nicest person on the planet who could never hurt a fly. You should've known it's not your place to just swoop in." Alpine gestured harshly. "You need to back off."

Jodi found her voice. "Isn't that something Rae should decide?"

"You say that like there's any chance at all. News flash! They aren't your friend! They *hired* you to do a job, and you took it as a sign to worm your way into someone's life. Forcing yourself on a camping trip, conveniently running into us here—"

"That was not on purpose, and Rae was giving me the opportunity to actually explain myself, which is something almost nobody does—"

"Yeah, well, that's Rae. You deal with thousands of reactive dogs, you get patient. Wait for them to stop biting and barking long enough to get them done and off the table."

Jodi was dizzy, and found herself saying the only thing she could to defend the scrap of dignity she had left. "I think you're jealous."

Alpine looked ready to kill. "I don't like you buzzing around. I never did, since the moment I found you digging in my trash. But I'm not jealous, because I know Rae a lot better than you. Rae burns out doing free grooms because they feel *pity* for the animals no one wants—"

Jodi liked to think she could hold her own in an argument. But the truth was, she was always the one begging for it to end. And so, she did the one thing she couldn't do with Vicki.

Without a word, she turned heel and walked, leaving Alpine mid-sentence.

"You said your piece," she told herself as she walked. "Enough is enough."

* * *

Her door was unlocked, and she panicked before remembering the drywall guy. His van was no longer in the driveway, so he'd let himself out. After making sure her computer was still safe under her desk, she examined the new wall. The expanse of white replacing the rippling plastic and dusty, cobwebby void was strange to see after so long, and she rubbed a hand over it.

Her cellphone rang, and her heart sped up, until she saw her mother's profile on the screen.

After a patient wait as her mother went on about Evelyn the Zumba Instructor in a badly disguised attempt to persuade Jodi into another date ("you know, she's quite *sensual* as she dances") Jodi asked, "Did you get my message?" She walked into her laundry room, ignoring the cold mugs of coffee on the counter.

"Oh, yes. I gave away your dad's sports equipment months ago."

Jodi squeezed her eyes shut. "I wish you'd asked me." She knelt and opened the mini fridge.

"Oh, I'm sorry, sweetheart. I figured you wouldn't want any of that stuff, you always hated the hobbies he tried to get you into." There was some hope in her voice, as though thinking Jodi had uncovered, deep down, her grief for the man.

"I was going to sell it online." Several lychee drinks were gone. Jodi hadn't expected the drywaller to take her seriously, and gloomily grabbed one of the two that remained.

"Oh." Her mother's tone was deflated. "Sweetheart, are you behind on your bills?"

"A bit."

"Well, you know what I'm going to say. Your bedroom's always here. You just have to move Dad's paperwork and books around to make room."

Jodi envisioned her old room, packed to the gills with her father. The thought of moving back in there, sleeping in the smell of her anxious childhood, actually sent a wave of nausea through her.

But the writing was on the wall. The wide, white expanse of it. "I might have to. For a bit. Until I get a few new clients." She stood and cracked open the lychee drink.

"Freelancing...always tough. It's why your father was always on your case about job security."

"He wasn't on my case." Jodi took a drink of the lychee, hoping it'd clear the fuzziness from the beer. "He just loved to point out the negatives whenever I was excited about something." Jodi didn't mean for the bitterness to slip out, but couldn't help it.

Her mother cleared her throat. "Well, sweetie, he was just looking out for you."

"No, he wasn't. He was annoyed whenever I tried something he was unfamiliar with. Made him feel less manly." Jodi wandered into her bedroom and flopped on her bed, the floss bouncing around her.

"I think you're being a bit hard on him." Her mother had that nervous tone.

"I'm not. He didn't like when either of us did anything out of the norm—it annoyed him." Jodi grabbed a floss packet and stared at it. "Did you ever consider recording him?"

"What do you mean?"

Jodi's tongue was lubricated by the beer. "Like, when he was in one of his rants. Whenever he sensed you got a bit too happy and spent hours putting you down, in that casual way of his."

"Why would I do that, Jodi?"

"I don't know. To show him later." She took a drink of lychee. "Or to show other people."

"I would never show anyone anything like that. That would have been an awful thing to do."

"He'd have been ripped apart online, you know. For things he didn't even consider were bad." Jodi rolled over. "You know, I just wish he'd have lived long enough to see me be called an abuser online. He'd have been one of the only people on Earth who wouldn't believe it for a second. 'That's a load, even if girls could be abusers,' he'd say. 'Jodi's too big a wimp.'"

"Sweetheart..." Her mother struggled to find something to say. She'd spent thirty years agreeing with her husband. Jodi was being cruel, expecting her mother to join in on her daughter's bitter train of thought. The moment her mother started agreeing with Jodi was the moment she would have to turn back and gaze at all the years she'd spent half-happy. "I think you're holding yourself back. If you dwell, all people will see is your sadness, and your past. That's what happened with Evelyn, I'm sure—"

"Mum. Please." Jodi pinched the bridge of her nose. "Please stop telling me to get over what happened, because I won't. I'm allowed to be angry and bitter."

"I'm not saying you aren't—"

"No, but what you're saying is that I should package myself all nice and pretty so *someone* will take me, like I'm a damaged bit of freight. If I can't be in a relationship with someone who knows me completely and accepts it anyway, then to hell with it, I might never have another relationship." Jodi realized how over-excited she was getting—she was waving the lychee drink around. Her words weren't just for her—she wanted her mother to hear them for herself. "Except...I might have a cat." She put the can safe on the bedside table.

"Oh?"

"Yeah." Jodi rested the phone on her face. "Sorry."

"That's alright, sweetheart." Her mother had that warm, slightly nervous tone that signified a phone call later to make sure Jodi wasn't angry at her. A holdover from her husband's sour silent treatments. "A cat?"

"Yeah, it's a long story..." Jodi fell back, and her head hit the mattress. "Oof." Bemused, she sat up and looked down.

"What happened?"

Frowning, Jodi checked down the side of the bed. "My pillow's not here."

"Did you leave it at, um...a friend's?"

"No, Mother." Jodi lifted the duvet, and a few of the floss packets slid to the floor. "Damn, I just made a mess. I've got to go."

After hanging up, Jodi resumed her bed search, shaking everything out. An under-the-bed glance ruled out the possibility that she'd unknowingly kicked it, though she knew it wasn't likely. Jodi slept still as a corpse; the only time the pillow left the bed was when she changed the case.

Now frustrated, Jodi stood on the bed and observed the room from above. Aside from noticing how dusty her overhead light was, she saw nary a corner of the pillow.

Had she brought it camping? No. She'd used the tent bag stuffed with her jacket, and then the hemorrhoid pillow. Yearning for her pillow was one of many things she'd thought about that long, uncomfortable night. Still, Jodi jumped off the bed and headed for the living room, where she'd unloaded her camping stuff. Perhaps she'd brought it and simply forgot to use it.

A search of the stuff revealed nothing. From there, Jodi upturned her entire suite, growing more and more frustrated. Misplacing things wasn't uncommon for her, but this wasn't a mug forgotten on the back of the toilet. Her pillow was one of the only constants in her life. It had comforted her more than her own parents, and its main characteristic was that it *didn't move.*

A bang upstairs made her jump a foot. The oddness of the situation made her twitchy, and she breathed a sigh as the familiar *shushuh, shushuh* of the treadmill bled through the ceiling.

Then Jodi frowned. Mr. Doucette could get into her suite. Was there any logical reason he'd broken in and taken her pillow? Was this a new technique of getting rent? It would certainly work. Mr. Doucette was odd enough, and there hadn't been anyone else in the—

Jodi's hands were, suddenly, cold.

There *had* been someone in the suite.

Memories of the drywall man asking her questions, smiling with easy confidence, filled her brain. The disappointment on his face when she'd left.

Her door was unlocked. Just because the van was gone...

Her skin was tingling horribly, and the rooms around her were suddenly looming and dark and filled with unfamiliar shapes. Real fear and revulsion gripped her, and with a burst of adrenaline Jodi ran to the door that led upstairs.

Then she stopped, hand on the knob. Behind the door was the one place she hadn't checked. The perfect place to hide, perhaps using the pillow to sit on and wait for Jodi to go to sleep.

Jodi let go of the knob and backed away, her heart in her throat. After fumbling backwards until she reached the door to outside, she flung it open and ran up the cold concrete steps.

The gravel path was hard on her bare feet, and the pain nearly brought tears to her eyes as she circled the house. After limping up the wooden steps, Jodi knocked hard on Mr. Doucette's front door.

It took a few tries before he finally cracked the door open, dressed in his grey sweatsuit, forehead shining with sweat. "Is the house on fire?" His enlarged eyes fell to her feet. "What in the hell."

Breathlessly, Jodi told him about the staircase, and Mr. Doucette stepped aside so she could pass. "Is this that same nutcase you were hiding from a few days ago?"

Jodi couldn't believe it had been less than a week since meeting Rae. "No, Rae's...fine. It was the drywaller who came to fix the hole."

"Was that today?" Coughing and clearing his throat, Mr. Doucette lumbered to the door that led to the staircase. Jodi's heart was pounding as, with no hesitation, Mr. Doucette pulled the door open, flicked on the switch, and peered down the stairs. "No one there."

Jodi let out a breath. "Can you see a pillow?"

"A pillow?"

"He took my pillow."

"Run of the mill freak, then. Getting his kicks from a girl's natural musk."

Jodi disliked greatly that final sentence. "How do I know he hasn't poisoned my food? Maybe he figured out that the window doesn't lock. Can I call the police?"

"This isn't Mayberry, girl—they won't give two shits about a stolen pillow."

"Well, can you give me the name of the company you hired?"

Mr. Doucette went to his fridge, upon which were tacked countless fliers and take-out menus. Jodi noticed a funeral card—*Annabelle Doucette.*

Mr. Doucette located a card, unstuck it from underneath a pack of McDonald's coupons, and handed it to Jodi. "Maybe it's best you kept that cat of yours."

"I..." Jodi trailed off, clutching the card. "How did you know I had one?"

"All girls who live alone get a cat." He pulled that old grey sock from a pocket and wiped his mouth. "Suppose you could use the comfort after dealing with that nutbar for as long as you did."

Jodi stared at the old man as he hacked another cough into the sock. "Vicki?"

"Yeah. Damn insane, that one. Could hear her through the vents. Wailing, screaming, banging around. Thought you were killing her at first, but you'd have to kill her damn near every night. Then in the mornings she's all dressed up and grinning, no hair out of place, with you looking like polished shit."

"Oh."

Mr. Doucette frowned and scratched his cheek. "You're looking better these days. Still a little rough."

"Thanks. I wouldn't know, I don't look in mirrors much."

"Might want to make a habit of it." Mr. Doucette sat in an armchair. "Was happy as hell when she took off. Told me once to get out of the way so she could film herself—I was watering my roses. Sprayed her a bit and she nearly called the cops. Would take a cat over that screwy broad any day of the week."

It was beyond disorienting, hearing someone say anything negative about Vicki. At best, they'd inevitably turn into the Devil's Advocate—like Jodi's mother, or Harper.

Yet, despite everything, there was a flash of instinctual revulsion at Mr. Doucette's crass assessment. Like everyone online, Mr. Doucette didn't know the whole story.

No one ever would. Just as Vicki's bad parts were hidden from the internet, her good parts couldn't be heard through the wooden floors, and a not-insignificant part of Jodi hated it. Hated that the story necessary to clear her own name had to be taped over all the bits of Vicki that made Jodi love her.

Mr. Doucette would never know the jokes between them. How Vicki would find a way to compliment every part of Jodi when she was feeling ugly. The late-night back scratches, and how she would make Jodi's Neo Citron the perfect temperature when she was sick. The good days. The many, many good days.

"She was passionate about her videos."

Mr. Doucette huffed. "People these days think they need to capture every second. My Belle would've been like that, if film was free. She always had the camcorder in my face." Mr. Doucette gestured to the boxes. "Now I've got boxes of tapes for furniture."

Surprised, Jodi took a closer look at the boxes labeled *Belle's Nonsense*. Lifting a lid revealed a mess of tapes and film boxes. "How many boxes of footage do you have?"

"Look around."

Jodi straightened up. "You could have it digitized. Then it wouldn't take up so much space."

"That ain't my wheelhouse. I can barely get my phone to work."

"What if I helped?" Jodi nudged a box. "This'll all expire sooner or later. You could keep these memories forever and be able to watch them whenever you wanted." Jodi had a thought. "There's also editing I could do, if you'd like me to condense and consolidate the clips."

Mr. Doucette stared at her like she'd grown a second head, then raised a hand. "I don't want charity."

"Well, it wouldn't be. I like helping out friends. Especially friends who give extensions on rent for a few months while I pay off a vet bill."

Mr. Doucette let that simmer for a moment. Then he let out a croaky, phlegmy laugh. "You kids kill me." Still chuckling, he ushered Jodi to the door, and it was only after it closed that Jodi realized she could've—and should've—taken the inside stairs.

Too embarrassed to knock again, she resigned herself to the painful walk over the path stones. Mr. Doucette's clearing of the stairwell made her feel a little better, but it didn't settle her nerves completely.

Jodi kept her eyes on the ground as she walked, trying her best to avoid the more painful rocks. So, just as she was approaching those cement steps to her suite, she didn't see anyone until a hand grabbed her arm from behind.

Chapter 11

Fear escaping her throat in a strangled scream, Jodi whirled around, her hand striking the person in the chest. With horror, Jodi watched Rae double up and wheeze.

"Oh no," was all Jodi could muster. She moved forward and, knowing it didn't help, patted Rae's shoulder. "Rae, I'm so sorry—"

Rae held up a finger, and after a few more breaths straightened up. "That would've been real bad if I was filming."

Jodi stepped back. "That's not funny."

"It's kind of funny."

"Why are you here?"

"Because you left." They held up a bag that Jodi hadn't noticed before. "Also, I keep meaning to give your robe back. It's been in my car for days."

Face red, Jodi took the bag. "Alpine didn't want me there. And I wasn't thrilled about hanging with her, either."

"I know." Rae paused, hand still on chest. "She's sure of what she saw."

Jodi nodded. "I've never had a good case. It's how it'll always be."

Rae said nothing for a few moments, then spoke in a slow, careful voice.

"Watching those videos was disorienting. I couldn't connect the two people in my brain. The person on that screen wasn't the same person I shared a tent with. I like to think I'm pretty good at sensing people—might come from working with animals. And you..." Rae screwed up their face in doubt. "Just wasn't adding up. I kept watching those videos, trying to find something that connected the two of you, and I couldn't.

"That is, until I heard you call Vicki a cunt for not cleaning properly." Rae pulled out their phone, tapped a few buttons, then held it up. From its tinny speakers came Jodi's voice, *"Scrub, you fucking cunt."*

Jodi's stomach twisted. "I don't remember saying that at all."

"I do."

Jodi stared. "I called you a cunt?"

"No. You called your *editing software* a cunt. You've said something like that, verbatim, when your timeline glitched and it didn't scrub forward when you wanted it to." Rae slipped the phone back into their pocket. "She recorded you getting mad at your computer and edited it into her video."

It was such a small thing. But somehow, it meant everything.

Jodi could never truly visualize Vicki constructing these videos—Jodi never had enough faith in her own memory to know which parts were edited. On the worst of robe nights, she wondered if the editing took place at all.

But now…now Jodi could finally see it. Vicki, standing over Jodi's shoulder, pretending to watch her edit, her phone silently recording Jodi's murmurs and curses. Then, later, importing the sound into the phone's editing app, cutting around it, using a declicker to remove the keyboard sounds…all the work it must have taken.

And, suddenly, the many, many good days seemed far away.

Jodi's eyes stung, and she fought a smile. "Thank you. For knowing me enough to catch that. I never did."

"You don't know yourself very well, Jodi."

She shrugged, tucking her arms around her torso as the cold evening air swirled. "I'm starting to get to know her again. Kinda like her."

"Yeah, she has her moments."

Jodi laughed, then swiped her running nose. "You should get back to Alpine."

"Nah. We had a disagreement, and she went home in a tiff."

"I hope it was about that damn photo wall, or something equally not about me."

"No, it was about you. She refused to even glance at your side, so I called her shallow and she called me a moron and we parted sourly."

Jodi closed her eyes briefly. "Rae, no."

"Rae, yes."

"The world is filled with people who will never believe me. I'm not going to let you take that on."

Rae surveyed her for a moment. "What're you going to do? Hit me?"

Jodi glared. "It's not *funny*."

"Beat me senseless?"

Jodi stepped forward and very half-heartedly smacked Rae's chest. Or, she tried to. Rae caught her limp wrist, then dragged her forward. Their lips met.

It was like she was floating a few inches off the ground when they parted. And it wasn't just because Jodi's feet were numb on the concrete. "Why'd you do that?" was the first thing that left her mouth.

"Because I wanted to. Have for a few days now."

Jodi's face was flaming. "It was the toilet mug that hooked you, wasn't it?"

Rae frowned, looking down. "Where are your shoes?" Immediately they grabbed Jodi's arm and guided her to the steps down to her door.

"Oh. You know. Drywaller took my pillow."

Rae's brows knitted. "Do you...wear your pillow on your feet?"

Inside, Jodi explained what had happened, sitting on the couch and warming her tender feet with her hands. She wasn't even finished when Rae left on their own search of the suite. Jodi listened as doors opened and closed, and remembered how she'd flipped out when Rae had accidentally glanced at her phone. Jodi had been afraid of Rae seeing even a glimpse of her. Now, a messy closet was nothing when they'd seen everything.

Rae returned empty-handed. "I'm staying here tonight."

Jodi sat up. "Excuse me? Do I have a choice?"

"Nope. I spent an hour scrolling through a shocking amount of comments wanting all kinds of creative punishments leveled at you. You're not staying alone." They pointed to the couch. "I'm sleeping here."

* * *

Jodi's heart wouldn't let her sleep. The exhaustion was there, behind her eyes, but her heart was pounding wetly in her chest; she could feel it under her night shirt, hear it in her ears.

With every soft movement in the other room, she'd jump. Though she knew it was Rae, she couldn't help the images of a masked intruder flashing in her imagination, and she could practically feel the gloved hand covering her mouth every time she closed her eyes.

Rae's presence did make her feel safer. However, it was half responsible for the sonorous performance in her chest. Their kiss replayed in her brain on an endless loop. Every time she was jerked awake by a noise, she expected the past day to have been a dream. Rae had kissed her—they had kissed her less than an hour after knowing her.

Jodi flipped over, the spare pillow unfamiliar under her head. It was better than the throw pillow Rae was using, and had assured her was fine; Jodi knew how many feather quills poked out. She knew, too, how hard and lumpy that couch was. Yet, she was too nervous to ask the obvious. The two of them had already slept in the same narrow cot—why was this more awkward?

Another flip, and she was staring at the dark ceiling. *This is stupid.*

After grabbing the newly washed robe and pulling it on, Jodi slipped out of bed and padded to the door.

The living room was lit dimly with the light of a phone. Jodi walked softly to the couch and discovered it empty of both Rae and the cushions. Both were, instead, on the floor; Rae was on their back, wrapped in a tiger-print blanket Jodi had dug from her packed closet, and was scrolling through their phone.

Rae hadn't, evidently, heard Jodi's door open, judging by the violence in which they jumped when Jodi asked, "Can't sleep?"

Rae cranked their head around. "Christ."

"Sorry. The couch is really bad. I was always the one sleeping on it after fights, so I know." Jodi sat on the cushionless frame.

"Never considered taking the cushions off, though."

"My legs are too long." Rae wiggled their socked feet, which stuck off several inches from the end of the cushions. "And the floor is somehow softer than that frame. I think whoever designed it must've moved onto those benches that repel homeless people."

"Which is a shame, because, y'know," Jodi affixed Rae with a serious look, "homeless people might just consider themselves the most important people in their own world, Rae."

That made Rae laugh, which made Jodi laugh. The two of them were giggling at three in the morning, their faces in horrible Halloween contrast from the phone light.

Then the rare smile faded from Rae's face. They jiggled the phone. "I'm trying to find the motorcycle guy."

"Oh?" Jodi leaned over to look at Rae's phone. "Any luck?"

"No. I checked all the social media my dad has."

"What about his hot tenting channel? People who commented a lot?"

"I checked." Rae rubbed an eye with a fist. "I've been through everything. The only one I found with a bike in the profile lives in Arizona."

"Bummer." Jodi sighed. "Well, old guys who enjoy motorbikes and being alone in the woods aren't exactly the biggest social media demographic."

"I'm not doing this anymore." Rae put their phone down.

"Yeah, I agree. You need sleep."

"I meant...I'm not going to look for him anymore."

Rae's eyes went to Jodi's. There was something in Rae's—something vulnerable. When Jodi said nothing, Rae continued. "The police and search people have the information, and they can do a helluva lot more with it. I know it's selfish. But I can't keep my life on hold for a grainy picture of a motorcycle. For a man who couldn't tell you my eye colour if you put a gun to his head."

Jodi chewed her lip in thought. "You know, I didn't cry at my dad's funeral."

"No?"

"No. He'd scoff if I cried in front of him, so I tried so hard not to. I cried at home after the funeral, but not for the reasons I should have. I was crying because I wanted to feel sadder. There wasn't the void media promised me when you lose a dad. Sometimes, I think he wanted it that way. I think being loved by a daughter was repulsive to him." Jodi put a hand on Rae's arm. "You're going to regret this. And that's okay, because regret is just another part of the Dead Dad Club."

A tear streaked down Rae's harshly shadowed cheek, and they used a shoulder to wipe it away. Another came, and Jodi cupped Rae's face before they could hide the tear again.

"I wanted him to see Noah's Bark." Rae's voice was small, and it was like Jodi could see the child, sitting there scrape-kneed on the couch cushion. "He might've been aggravating about it, but I still wanted him to see it." Rae let out a growl of frustration and scrubbed harshly at their eyes. "All right, I'm done."

Jodi swallowed, then glanced around. "You know, this room is probably filled with drywall dust. You shouldn't be sleeping in it."

"Oh, great. Glad I knew that three hours ago."

Jodi pulled a feather from the awful throw pillow. "For your health, you should probably...you know, sleep in another room."

Their eyes met, Jodi gave a weak grin, and understanding dawned on Rae's face. "Oh. Right. Um. If you think it's safer."

Jodi helped Rae to their feet, grabbed the pillow, then pulled them to the bedroom. "The bed is just a double, not a queen." Jodi fussed with the blankets. "I'm not sure if you have a preference of side, I usually start on the left but always drift diagonally, so don't hesitate to give my feet a whap back into place—"

Rae gently took her arm, pulled her in, and shut her up with another kiss. The embarrassment melted, and Jodi wrapped her arms around Rae's neck, fingers threading into the soft hair at the nape.

Then she pulled away. "I'm not a free groom, am I?"

Rae's eyes were glazed. "Again, that's just about the last thing I expected you to ask right now."

"I'm not someone you feel bad for, and that's why—"

Rae covered Jodi's mouth with a hand. "I'm revoking your right to speak. Shut up." Before Jodi could lick—an instinctual move—Rae dropped the hand and reeled her in again.

Tomorrow, things would get difficult again. The bad things weren't gone. There were people who would still glance with suspicion and pity. A man was somewhere unknown, maybe in the ink of the woods, absorbing into the cold autumn ground, rattail beads sinking into the dirt. Floss may still appear at her door, and her bank account wasn't any fuller. A cat slept fitfully without a leg, and several moles lived to wreak lawn havoc another day.

It didn't matter. Not then. They were safe in their pocket of night, in that cold bedroom with the failing pillow population, gently dusted with drywall.

Chapter 12

At seven the next morning, Jodi was making coffee. She'd managed to squeak every cupboard and bang her mug on several corners, but Rae remained unmoving in the bed. Jodi, ever the worrier, had waited with a hand on Rae's ribs until they moved with a breath, just to be positive they hadn't succumbed to the drywall dust. The reality was that the exhaustion of the last three weeks had simply caught up.

The two of them had kept the windows closed all night, just in case, and the suite was stuffy. Wanting fresh air, Jodi took her mug and slipped outside to sit on the concrete steps.

She was halfway through her mug when footsteps approached. Jodi looked up, and to her surprise saw Harper heading in her direction, cloak billowing.

"Get up." Harper took Jodi's arm and pulled her upright. For a wild moment Jodi thought Harper was going to start throwing punches, until she continued, "We're getting breakfast."

Jodi steadied her cup, which had nearly sloshed coffee down her front. "I don't really want—"

"I've got an hour until Evan's alarm." Harper affixed Jodi with a firm gaze. "Just come with me. I'm sick of us having conversations outside our houses, I feel like a fifties wife or something."

Jodi jerked a thumb over her shoulder. "I..." She trailed off. Now was not the time to tell Harper she had Rae in her bed. "Just one second, okay? I'm going to throw some pants on."

"Hurry up."

Back inside, Jodi hurriedly changed out of her hedgehog pajamas and into her overalls. Rae didn't move, and Jodi spent a few moments studying their relaxed face, wondering if she should wake them. Rae's eyes were still shadowed from lack of proper sleep, so Jodi decided to leave a note instead, explaining where she'd gone.

They slept with one hand curled under their chin, the other arm lying across Jodi's vacated spare pillow.

In the night, Jodi had found herself inching close to Rae when sleeping, and had woken up pressed against their chest, fingers tracing the lighthouse tattoo. It had been so long since Jodi had woken up happy.

* * *

Jodi thought Harper was joking until she put the parking brake on. "Why are we here?" Jodi asked, eyes on the sign above the restaurant.

"I wanted to go someplace nice." Harper grabbed her purse and opened her door. "You said this was a cloth napkin place, and they do breakfast. The crêpes look yummy."

Jodi's mouth was suddenly dry. "To be honest, Harper, I don't know if I should be spending a whole lot on breakfast right now. With the vet bill—"

"No, girl, I'm paying. Don't worry about it."

Unable to think of another excuse, Jodi exited the car and followed Harper towards the restaurant she'd dined-and-dashed from weeks earlier. If she were more cynical, she'd suspect Harper was doing this on purpose as revenge for their argument.

The waiter probably wouldn't work mornings. It'll be fine.

The moment they entered, Jodi's eyes hit a bulletin board behind the hostess stand. It was tacked with grainy security screenshots surrounding a little "Walkouts will be prosecuted" sign. And there, freshly tacked, was Jodi's plaid mackinaw.

Jodi tucked her chin into her sweater and kept head down as they were seated.

Immediately, Jodi lifted the menu to shield her red face.

Harper took a sip of water, then spoke. "I don't like how we ended our conversation yesterday." She let out a nervous breath. "You pushed me, and I said things. We both said things."

Jodi peeked over her menu, eyes scanning the heads in the restaurant, praying she recognized no one. "I know."

Harper seemed comforted by Jodi's agreement. "I feel bad about the whole Vicki thing. I wasn't able to explain my perspective right. I know there's always three sides, so I just want to be neutral, you know?" Harper laid a hand on the table. "The most important thing is that it's all in the past." Her assurance with the final words seemed practiced—like this was a well-worn phrase. Jodi imagined her saying it to Evan the night before, in the stiff, formal, after-fight debrief.

Their waitress set down their coffees, and Jodi used the mug to hide the bottom of her face. "Are things fixed with Evan?"

"It's looking a bit better." Harper circled the top of her mug with a finger. "Listen. I'm thinking of giving you a bit of cash to help with that cat. I know you're embarrassed to admit your money issues, but I know this would help. The trap shouldn't have been above ground like that."

Jodi let out a breath. "That's really nice of you—"

"And I was hoping," Harper continued, "that you could do me a favour."

Jodi's gratitude dampened. "Oh?"

Surprisingly, Harper's face was as flushed as Jodi's felt. "It's a really small thing. Not even a favour, just more of an invitation."

Jodi stared at her friend, who seemed to have trouble gathering her thoughts. Her eyes were still shadowed underneath—Jodi realized only now how much her friend had wilted over the years.

"Evan and I were talking—well, arguing—all night," Harper continued. "Finally we landed on an idea to help us get over this little bump. It's certainly a creative solution."

Jodi waited, with Harper saying nothing. "What is it?" Jodi finally asked.

"It's, well…" Harper gestured to Jodi.

"Me? What about me?"

"You would join us." Harper's face was very red. "In bed."

There was real danger that Jodi's mug would slip from her fingers—she redoubled her grip as she gaped at Harper.

"It'll be safe," Harper insisted. "It's the best solution. I know Evan—he'll sulk about the Buckerfield's guy unless he gets even somehow, and there's a few women in his pickleball league I've been nervous about. This way I know it's not really cheating, because he can't continue an affair. You'll have a fun night, plus have some cash to pay that vet bill. Everyone wins." Harper poked Jodi playfully, a forced smile on her face. "C'mon, you've probably been dying to kiss me for years, don't lie. And I'll knock something off my bucket list."

Jodi was still struggling to find something to say. Finally, she managed to get words out. "So you guys would be...paying me for sex?"

"No!" Harper bit her lip. "Well, a little. I would be. Evan wouldn't know. He'd be less willing if he thought you weren't into it, so you'll have to enjoy yourself." Harper waved a hand. "I just...I'd feel better if this was transactional, at least between us. You can't tell him about the money."

Jodi found her head shaking, out of her control. "I don't think I can do it."

"Yes, you can." There was desperation in Harper's smile.

"I'm seeing someone."

"Who? Shit Hawk? Jodi, you've known them a week, you're still free game."

"I don't want to be. I don't see you— either of you—that way."

Harper's smile dropped. "You don't find me attractive?"

"Not in that way! You don't find me attractive in that way, either."

"I think I'm seeing everyone that way, these days." Harper rubbed her eyes with her fingers. "My mind is in pieces. The only thing that scares me more than losing Evan is having to spend the rest of my life with him.

It's like I'm fighting against a door, but I can't tell if I'm forcing it open or trying to keep it shut." Harper, suddenly, put a hand on Jodi's, her red eyes alight. "What if we ran away? You wanted to leave before. Go to Scotland. We could do it together. A long vacation. We both want to escape this town—what if we actually did? Went someplace no one knew us? Just take off, like Thelma and Louise."

Jodi's stutter was interrupted by someone stopping at their table. Her gaze locked onto a familiar pair of thick, neon yellow glasses.

Any hope that the waiter didn't recognize Jodi was dashed by the gleeful indignation in his eyes. "Good morning, ladies. How are we doing on this stunning Saturday morning?"

Harper cleared her throat, retreated her hand, and sat back into her chair. "We're fine. We might need a few more minutes with the menu."

The waiter's eyes slid to Jodi's again. "I'm afraid we won't be able to serve you two breakfast this morning."

Jodi pushed her mug away. "Harper, let's go."

"Why?" Harper's eyes were fiery as she glared at the waiter. "Are you...like...actually discriminating against us?"

The waiter was momentarily offended. "What? No, of course not, we are a completely inclusive restaurant." He cleared his throat. "But we have reason to believe your date had dined and dashed a few weeks ago." He lifted his hand. Between two fingers was the photo from the bulletin board.

Jodi had suffered her share of mortification; this was just one more in a long list. Yet, the sight of that photograph—another of her lowest moments, captured and displayed for the world to see—lit in her a deep sense of *enough is enough*.

She set down her coffee cup and met the waiter's gaze. "I don't think that's me."

His eyebrows went up. "I'm fairly certain it is."

"Jodi, you dined and dashed?" Shock glazed Harper's face.

"No, someone with a faint resemblance to me dined and dashed." Jodi held out a hand. "And I can prove it. Give me the picture."

Curiosity and surprise lit the waiter's formerly smug expression, and he passed the photograph to Jodi, who studied it closely. Despite the bad quality, she could see how scared and miserable she looked, sneaking out of the building.

Jodi stood. "Thelma? Shall we?"

Harper's face went through several layers of confusion before it finally cleared. She stood, and the two women inched past the now startled waiter.

"Wait." He fell in step behind them. "You have to stop."

"He can't legally tackle us," Jodi muttered to Harper.

The two women left the restaurant, the waiter still following behind. He could only keep saying *wait* in a defeated tone as Jodi and Harper got in the car. They pulled out of the restaurant parking lot, him fading in the rearview.

"Take the back way home, past the unhoused camp." Jodi slumped in her seat. "It's busier there, just in case that guy follows us in his waitermobile."

Harper's face was shocked. "You said she didn't pay, but never told me you didn't, either."

Jodi sighed. "I also never told you that I dumpster dove for a broken pet crate."

Her head snapped around. "Did you take my bag of cans?" Jodi winced. "I was wondering about those! I assumed a homeless person took them. I was imagining it buying a hot meal, not a case of that weird-ass lychee drink."

"In all fairness, you bitched about returning those cans every time we hung out. Plus, you haven't paid me for half the coffees I pick up. It was justified." Jodi peeked out the window. "Any cops?"

"How has your life gotten so grungy?"

"My life has been grungy for a while." Jodi cranked her head around to look at her friend. "I'm a mess, bud. It's nothing to be jealous about." She studied the printed photograph in her hand. Her own tired, scared face in grainy black and white. She crumpled it up. "The grass isn't greener."

"Then why do you seem less bummed?"

Jodi stared, taken aback, still scrunched down in her seat. "I am?"

Harper nodded. "You're different. Even different from when Vicki was around, and things were good. It's a general vibe I can sense. A chiller vibe. Before, I always imagined you as a cat a couple microseconds before booking it up a tree."

Jodi touched her face. "I haven't done anything different."

"No, it's just your vibe. Ever since that Rae person showed up at your door." Harper pulled into a thrift store parking lot, stopped the car, and faced Jodi. "I'm going to say something hard for me, okay? As long as we're being honest?"

"Okay?"

"I didn't like Shit Hawk because I was jealous."

"I know. You already said you were jealous of my objectively fabulous single life—"

"I was jealous of Rae."

Jodi stared. Harper's eyes shone, and her nose was red, despite her trying to smile.

"But they aren't *feeling* feelings, Jodi. They're feelings that manifest when your leg is caught in a trap. I'm so desperate for something else that I'm covetous of a platonic friend who dumpster dives and steals my cans for rent, just because she pays attention to me."

"I think that's a bit harsh—"

"I'm jealous because we've known each other for years, and it takes two days for some random stranger to capture your attention." She smacked the wheel with a hand, hard. "And then I think, fuck, what if it's just me? What if I'll never be happy with what I have, and grasp at whatever's far away? I just wander through life, wishing for better grass with no fucking moles in it."

Jodi's tongue was stuck. No words came out for several moments. Then, finally, "I can't give you what you want, Harper. You don't even know what you want. You just know it's not this." She reached out to put a hand on Harper's arm, then thought against it. "No marriage was fixed with a threesome, Harper. It's not even a Band-Aid solution, it's just grinding that dirt in the wound."

"What about a twosome?" Harper's red eyes held no hope.

It didn't matter whether this was a case of unrequited love, or an unchecked item on a bucket list—both possibilities left Jodi hollow. She shook her head.

Harper faced forward. A tear tracked down her cheek.

Jodi's phone buzzed in her pocket.

"You can take that." Harper passed a hand over her face. "I think I need a minute alone."

Jodi nodded, then got out of the car and walked to the roadside to answer.

It was the drywall company. Jodi explained why she was calling, and the receptionist's response was dumbfounded. "Todd wasn't carrying any pillow when he returned the keys to the van. And no one found a pillow in there today."

"Oh." Jodi thought hard. "Maybe he just hid it. Or stuffed it under his shirt."

"I didn't notice any sudden weight gain in him, either." The woman sounded on the edge of laughter. "I'm sorry about your pillow. But I would bet money Todd didn't take it. He's not like that."

Jodi wished she could take apart that naive logic, but knew it wasn't appropriate. Instead, she thanked the woman and tapped *end*, disappointed and anxious and hollow.

Cars whizzed by before her, and she gazed down the road, at the sun coming up over the distant mountain.

* * *

Rae was awoken by the harsh buzz of a call. They slapped at an unfamiliar bedside table until they hit the phone and brought it to their face. It was an unfamiliar number. Rae tapped *answer*. "Hello."

"Is this Rae?" It was an unfamiliar woman's voice.

"Yes." Rae rolled over and noticed that the other side of the bed was empty. "Who's this?"

"My name is Harper, I'm Jodi's neighbour. I got your number from a business card she had in her purse."

Rae's stomach tightened with a strange fear, and they were suddenly sitting upright. "What's going on? Why is she out with you?"

"I dragged her out to have breakfast with me. We were talking in a parking lot, she stepped out of the car for a second, and now she's gone."

"Gone?" Heart was thundering. "What do you mean, *gone*?"

"I know it's nothing, she probably just went for a short walk to clear her head—we were having a pretty heavy conversation—but I've been calling her name, and she's not picking up the phone, and I can't see her anywhere in the street—"

This can't be happening. Not again. "Where are you?"

"Just at the thrift store, five minutes away, near the homeless mission—"

* * *

Six minutes later, Rae pulled into the parking lot, just as Harper exited the thrift store. "They don't have public bathrooms, and she's not in the aisles," she called to Rae as they got out of the car.

"How long has she been gone?"

"Twenty-ish minutes. It's not long, but I know Jodi—she doesn't just wander off. She hates walking and she hates the cold."

"I know." Rae gazed down the long street, lined with make-shift shelters. Across the way was the train tracks. "Have you asked anyone where she went?"

"No."

"What was she wearing?"

"A champagne cardigan, not warm at all. That's why it's so odd she'd walk off."

Rae went up to a woman sitting quietly on a tall curb, wrapped in an old duvet. "Excuse me—have you seen a woman in a beige sweater pass by? Or...uh...get into a car, or anything?"

The woman shook her head, an apologetic look on her face.

Images of threatening comments on Vicki's videos kept up a tickertape in Rae's head. They focused on Harper. "You go down that way, I'll go up this way. Try to walk double her normal pace—it shouldn't be hard. If we can't find her in fifteen minutes, I'm calling the cops."

"She's fine, right?" Harper hitched her bag onto her shoulder. "I mean, she's only been gone twenty minutes—"

"I'm glad you're optimistic, but I'm not the kind of person who's assuming the best when someone disappears."

Harper's face blanched at the realization. With a jerky nod, she hurried down the street. Rae headed in the opposite direction, ignoring the ache in their ankle. *Please let this be embarrassing in five minutes.*

It had been a full two days before Rae had stopped assuming things were fine with their dad. The idea of his being missing was so bizarre, and the thought of Grant guffawing at Rae's overreaction was so unappealing, that Rae had denied their gut and assumed the best.

Rae wouldn't make the same mistake now. Even if it was embarrassing. Even if this panic made them cringe in the future. Because the thought of Jodi—this woman Rae hadn't even known about before reading her name in a notebook a week ago, this woman who wasn't even a friend—being torn from that future was pulling the air from their lungs.

Chapter 13

Jodi's dad had once locked her outside for an hour in the freezing rain.

Her mother was out visiting relatives for the night, and Jodi had endured a verbal browbeating from her father that had reduced her to tears. What it was about escaped her now—it was never anything significant enough to remember—but she did recall her father's irritation with her crying. He'd gotten so fed up that he ordered her outside to compose herself with a walk. Jodi hated walking—he knew this—but she did as she was told. Thinking she would only be outside for a few minutes, Jodi had donned a pair of soft moccasins and a sheer cardigan.

After her walk in the November drizzle that had started a few minutes in, Jodi had tried to go back inside, but the deadbolt was in place. She'd knocked, then rung the doorbell, then called for her father to open the door. A few minutes passed, and she did it again. The door didn't open.

Part of her was terrified that he'd had a heart attack, but the rational side of her knew this was on purpose. Her father hated

Jodi's softness. Yet, Jodi got the impression that he loved to test it. Her tears disgusted him, but the disgust never stopped him from pushing her until she broke. This was yet another warped test for whatever pseudo-strength he revered.

Jodi's moccasins were wet and freezing, and her toes were getting numb. Her damp cardigan did nothing to hold in warmth, and she was soon shivering. There was a biting wind that went through the porous material like it was nothing.

Her tears were cold on her cheeks, and she wanted so badly to knock on a neighbour's door and tell them what was going on, but the fear of her father's anger kept her in place. As a result, she didn't yell—she could only press her lips to the crack and beg for him to open the door.

It took fifty-five minutes before the door unlocked. Jodi didn't say a word as she stepped inside; she just hoped he could feel her hatred.

His excuse was that he'd accidentally locked it and had his headphones on, but she could see the truth in his eyes. Neither told Jodi's mother, and neither spoke of it again. But at fifteen, Jodi had felt a severing between them. She could forget the cold—it was the satisfaction and borderline amusement she'd seen in her father's eyes that did the cutting.

The memory played through Jodi's brain as she stood in the cold, damp parking lot. She had just ended the call with the drywall company and had decided to give Harper a few more minutes before returning to the car.

Jodi wrapped her sweater tighter around herself and gazed down the road at the many glistening tents and tarps. Suddenly, her missing pillow seemed so trivial. Jodi sighed, shook her head, and was about to head back to the car when something in the distance caught her eye. Something farther down the road, under the overpass.

Her heart jumped into her throat, and she was frozen to the blacktop. Then she was running, even as cars hit puddles and splattered her overalls and cardigan with muck, and her shoes soaked through with oily water. She ran towards the huge, spraypainted overpass, under which were a few abandoned tarps, many discarded bags of garbage, and a lone tent. A familiar brown tent, with a long chimney poking out the top, throwing up smoke.

* * *

Jodi stood outside the tent, her chest heaving. "Grant? Is that you?"

For one second, she thought she was wrong. This was simply another person with a hot tent and stove, or it was the result of Grant being robbed. But before she could continue with this train of thought, the tent unzipped, and Grant's grizzled head poked out, his bearded mouth popped open with surprise.

"Oh!" The surprise was replaced immediately with a guilty grin that Jodi recognized—it was there every time he arrived a half-hour late. "You caught me."

Relief and fury made her dizzy, and the world tilted. "Yes. I did." Not until that moment did Jodi realize just how strongly she'd assumed Grant was dead—him alive before her didn't feel real.

"How did you know it was me?"

Jodi gestured to the tent. "I'd recognize this contraption anywhere."

He unzipped the door fully. "Come in, come in—it's about time you see the inside in person." Jodi bent down and stepped inside, greeted by the now familiar heat and the musk of unshowered man. "Isn't the warmth lovely? Shocked, I bet."

She stood awkwardly, her head bent to accommodate the low ceiling. "Actually, no. I went hot tenting recently."

"Get out." Grant's eyes narrowed in jovial suspicion as he plopped down on his cot, crossing his dirty feet under him. "You did not."

"I did, because a friend of mine was missing, and it was a last-ditch effort to figure out what happened."

"Well, isn't that something."

Jodi stared at Grant. She stared until Grant's expression went from curiosity to annoyance. "What's that scathing look for? C'mon, kid, out with it—I'm not a mind reader."

"Grant, you've been missing for almost three weeks! Search parties were out looking, and your kid's been worried sick."

Grant froze, staring at Jodi. Then that guilty grin cracked his face. "What?"

Jodi explained the entire story. She spent longer on it than was necessary—shock made her stutter and ramble. Grant listened, but that grin never left. "Have you been here this entire time?" Jodi finished. Grant jerked a shrug, which meant *yes.* "Why? Why, oh why?"

"Jodi..." Grant shook his head. "You have no idea the life these homeless people have. It's been eye-opening. It's a whole other level."

It was then Jodi's turn to listen as Grant went on about his time spent pretending to be homeless. "I think we should all try walking in their broken, disgusting shoes, just once in our lives," he concluded. "It'll be a revelation for the phonies of the world." He held up a finger. "It took me losing my keys to realize that our houses are one mistake from being uninhabitable. Think about it, kid—your cushy life indoors is hanging by a thread."

"You did this because you lost your keys?" Jodi wished it was legal to strangle an old man. "Why didn't you call a locksmith?"

Grant waved an impatient hand.

"Why didn't you call *Rae?*"

Grant blew a raspberry. "I sent a text. Never answers me—got too busy a life for their old man."

"Did you?" Jodi held out a hand. "Let me see."

Grant sighed and handed over the phone. Jodi tapped at the screen. "Is this in airplane mode?"

"Yeah, I put it like that so it doesn't wake me up. Hard enough to fall asleep with the sound of the damn overpass." Grant picked up a piece of wood and chucked it into the stove. "I usually keep my phone off anyway, but I needed it for filming. It's almost out of juice, though—I'll need to make another trip to the thrift store to charge my power bank. They don't let you use the damn bathroom, but you can sneak an outlet." Grant tapped the power bank on the ground. "I'm telling you, this is going to be a *hell* of a video. It'll be worth it, even if I haven't had edamame for three weeks."

Jodi went to Rae's chat and saw the singular text Grant had sent. *Get my spare keys and pick up my truck from my campsite in the mountains. Had to get a ride home with Lenny, pal from my Tai Chi class. Couldn't sit around and wait for you to be out of party mode.* A tiny exclamation point was next to the message, indicating that it had failed to send. Jodi's heart hammered. "You do realize that texts don't send or receive in airplane mode, right?"

Grant glanced at the screen. "No, it sends. It's right there."

Jodi tapped the little airplane icon. Immediately, texts and missed calls came pouring in.

Grant winced. "See, that's why I keep it off."

Jodi watched the message icon tick up. "People thought you were dead."

Grant let out a barking laugh and lay back on the cot, folding his hands under his head. "Well, that's an overreaction, Christ. We're too damn connected these days. A guy can't even get a few days to himself."

Jodi put down the phone. "So you're mad at Rae for living their life without being at your beck and call, but you find it appropriate to fuck off without telling anyone?"

Grant didn't say anything for a moment, his eyes shocked. "Excuse me. I did tell—"

Jodi tapped the phone. "This message said nothing, even if it did go through. You could've died on the roadside for all this message says."

Grant's face was getting red. "I don't have to tell people anything. I'm a grown man, and I'd appreciate if you don't talk to me like I'm a child, kid."

"Then don't act like one." Jodi was so furious that her instinctual cowing under an angry gaze was gone. "All Rae wanted was to do right by you, and they've been working their ass off—"

"Aw, Rae is fine. Good for them to get a kick in the pants. Going off thinking they're too good for their old man—this shows Rae what's truly important." Grant pulled a hand from beneath his head and gestured with it. "Look at these hobos. Families have abandoned them completely. They know what it's like." With a grunt, Grant twisted in the cot to face the tent wall. "Whatever. Get out of here, kid. I'd like to be alone."

Jodi stood, and was about to leave when something caught her eye. She reached forward and with one angry tug, yanked the pillow from beneath Grant's head. He yelped and twisted around, eyes shocked.

"How dare you break into my house." Jodi brandished her pillow. "You think you can just do whatever you want, no matter who it inconveniences?" The words burst from her, on instinct. "*We don't do that here, Grant.*"

Grant was red with embarrassment, but his jaw was set. "Guess I do. Should've locked the door."

"That's not going to hold up in court."

"What are you going to do? Call the cops for grand theft pillow? You're dreaming." Grant turned over again. "Place is too big for you. You're living the cushy life, working from home on that big, fancy computer. Try living outdoors for a night, kid. It'll change your perspective on things."

Jodi tried to calm her breathing. "In twenty minutes, I'm going to tell Rae you're alive. You can call them before that if you want to explain yourself."

Grant didn't turn. "I don't have to explain shit."

"Rae sacrificed their new business to look for you. It's the least you could do."

Grant glanced over his shoulder, a skeptical look on his face. "What business?"

Breathe, Jodi. "Just call them." In that moment, she realized just how long it had been since leaving Harper's car—she must be baffled. Jodi had been so overwhelmed by the sight of the tent, she hadn't even sent a text.

Her hand went to her pocket for her phone. It wasn't there. Dread in her throat, Jodi searched the dirt around her, not seeing the phone.

"How do you even know my kid?"

Jodi was done talking. She roughly exited the tent, the flap slapping her in the face on the way out.

The phone wasn't outside the tent, either. Logic told her what her gut feared— her phone had bounced out of her pocket while she ran. The cardigan's pockets were shallow, wide, and structureless—perfect for letting things escape.

"Great," she muttered as she started the walk back, eyes on the ground, searching desperately. Harper was in a delicate state— what if she assumed Jodi had taken off like a coward after Harper's vulnerable confession? Taken off *and* refused to answer her phone. *Just great.*

Things got worse when she arrived at the thrift store parking lot—still phoneless—and Harper's Jetta was gone. She rotated in desperation, searching for the car, and seeing nothing. "Harper!" She stomped her foot on the ground. "Why!"

It was at this moment when her stomach gave that telltale indication. The one that said, *you've had two cups of coffee this morning, bucko. Buckle up.*

There was no other option. Knowing the apparent iron-grip the thrift store had on their bathroom key, Jodi headed, on foot, towards her house—back the way she came. With any luck, she'd find her phone the second time passing. If not, she was a half hour from her own toilet, and could only pray for a public bathroom along the way.

* * *

There was an A&W with a bathroom available at the eleventh hour. Jodi occupied the stall for at least twenty minutes, nerves and coffee having done a number on her digestion. The entire time she cursed Harper—for the café coffee, and for driving off at the first indication of Jodi wandering away like an adventuresome toddler.

Once finished, Jodi continued on home. The last part of the walk was a steep incline, and Jodi's curses became her mantra as she powered up, legs itching and lungs aching. She had never spent more time away from her heating pad in her life.

A car passed her, and she watched with envy as it sped up the hill. Her envy morphed into surprise when the car's brake lights went on, and the car came to an abrupt halt, stuttering over the wet pavement. Her surprise grew as the car began reversing, maneuvering to the roadside.

She stopped walking and watched as the car approached. It took too long to realize that the car was a familiar silver Hyundai.

"Dammit," Jodi muttered, envisioning Rae missing her note and, with the assumption that Jodi had rudely left without explanation, decided to return to their own bed. Then she realized Rae had been going in the wrong direction, heading back to Jodi's. *What's going on?*

The car stopped, and Rae jumped out and circled the car, jogging in Jodi's direction. "Sorry," Jodi called, "I wanted to get back before you woke—"

Rae cut off Jodi's words by grabbing her upper arm and yanking her into a hug, crushing her against their chest.

Jodi realized what must have happened. "You found out, huh?" She returned the hug. "I'm so relieved. Pissed, but relieved."

"Pissed but relieved is exactly how I'm feeling, yes." Rae's tone was strangled and angry. "What the hell, Jodi?"

Jodi blinked, face pressed into Rae's shoulder. "What?"

"I called the police—"

"Wait, wait, *what?*" Jodi pulled back, searching Rae's face. "Okay, yeah, he's a moron, but he didn't break any laws other than the pillow theft, and I really don't care about that—he said he had no idea about everything else, and he's an idiot enough where I believe him—"

As Jodi yammered, a stressed and staring Rae lifted their hands to grip their hair in confusion. Finally, they once more pressed a hand against Jodi's mouth, cutting off her flow of words. "Jodi," Rae said, "I have zero idea what you're talking about."

Jodi blinked, unable to talk around the hand. She reached up and pulled it away. "Wait. Why did you call the cops?"

"Because you've been *missing for an hour,* you idiot!" Rae dug in their pocket and pulled out—

"My phone!" Jodi exclaimed with relief, accepting it gratefully. "Where was it?"

"On the side of a very dangerous road. You know—thrown there in the same way traffickers dispose of girls' phones after snatching them off the street." Rae took Jodi's shoulders and shook them. "Why why why why why. Why would you do this to me?"

Jodi took the shaking with grace. "I'm sorry." The irony was only hitting her then—

the horror grew. "God, I'm really sorry. But I have an extremely good explanation."

Rae stopped shaking her, but still gripped her shoulders. "Is it something to do with Mini Wheats losing a leg when I wasn't looking?"

Jodi blinked. "How did you know that?"

"You got a phone call, and you have no position to be mad about me answering, either—I was expecting a call from someone's trunk. But it was just the vet, saying she could go home."

Jodi beamed. "That's wonderful! Did she say anything about—"

"You. Hour. Where. And it better be a hell of an explanation."

Jodi faltered, realizing that Rae didn't know. Which meant Grant had not called or texted, waiting—again—for someone else to take care of the problems he created. Jodi felt there was no explanation like a simple one, so she grabbed Rae's face, looked them in the eye, and said, "Your dad has been living as a homeless man."

Rae stared at her, eyes impassive. Then the emotions flicked across at rapid speed, and Jodi knew she didn't have to explain a thing. Rae knew their dad—and all the pieces were falling into place.

Finally, Rae exhaled hard. "You know, the thing about the homeless..."

"They might just consider themselves the most important people in their own world."

Rae nodded. Then they closed their eyes and pressed their forehead against Jodi's. "I'm very glad you haven't been kidnapped. That's all I'm going to say right now, because I feel if I say anything else I might just scream."

Jodi smiled, then pressed her cold lips to Rae's.

Epilogue

"You've been lying down all day, Miss Tripod." Jodi took two remaining legs and made them dance, Mini Wheats watching her reproachfully. "Why haven't you skittered around this morning like a tiny monster yet?"

Mini Wheats let out a *brrp* of argument.

"Yes, I know. You've already had plenty of exercise in the yard. You'll get a mole one day, don't worry."

She looked past the cat to Rae, squished in the corner of the couch by Jodi taking up more than her half. They'd turfed the old, lumpy couch and replaced it with one a lot comfier, but much smaller; they needed room for the massive record player cabinet Jodi insisted Rae keep, on which they kept Jodi's dad's collection on rotation. It didn't matter if the couch was small. No one ever slept on it.

"Rae, I've got a long day of editing ahead. Mr. Doucette still thinks his wife's footage of the neighbour's tomatoes can somehow make an award-winning independent film, and I intend on proving him right before Christmas."

Rae tapped on the laptop they'd finally bought. "Sorry. I thought the email would come sooner. Sit up."

Jodi struggled her way into a proper seating position. "All this secrecy. Makes me nervous."

"It's a good thing."

"Yes, but it still makes me nervy."

"Shut up. I want to watch this before work."

"God, how long is it?"

"We don't have to watch the whole thing." Rae lifted a grumpy Mini Wheats from Jodi's lap and set the computer down in her place. "Just a few minutes, so you get the gist. Or you could just look at the title."

Jodi looked down at the screen. And then she froze. "I know this channel."

"Yes, I know. Very popular internet sleuth."

Jodi stared at the name of the video, unable to speak.

"It's unlisted." Rae tried to prevent Mini Wheats from climbing over their head and failed. "And it can stay that way. They signed a contract agreeing to take the gamble—I've given them a deposit in case you want this to stay buried forever, keep it just for you, and whoever you want to show. Or just to know it exists, somewhere."

The Framing of Jodi Marples.

"It's all there." Rae tapped the screen. "MatthewMysteryBox was great. Found so much evidence of editing—way more than either of us. It's clear as day. Went into her personal life, and yours—just enough to paint a true picture. Got some truly entertaining interviews from Mr. Doucette. No punches pulled on either side, but the truth favours you by a landslide. People will understand. That is, if you want to open up such an old wound." Rae pulled Mini Wheats from their head and chucked her onto the floor. Off she skittered clumsily for her food bowl, purring.

Rae took Jodi's cold hand. "It's up to you what goes online. If you want, I'll have Matthew delete it completely."

"No." Jodi swallowed, and a tear slipped down her cheek. She leaned against Rae, and they wrapped their arms around her shoulders. "Do I have time to think about it?"

"It'll stay unlisted for fifty years if you want."

Jodi nodded. Then Rae's phone buzzed, the lock screen with the familiar picture lighting up. She gestured. "You can take that, if you want."

"It's just Alpine with another question about the frigging blade sharpener guy." Rae grabbed the phone and went into another room. Jodi remained on the couch, her heart thrumming as she stared at the laptop screen.

It didn't matter, really. It could be posted, or it could remain unseen—what mattered was that the truth existed, there. It was real.

Jodi smiled, thinking about Rae's lock screen. It was Jodi, months ago, in the tent. A photo taken by Rae without her knowing. Jodi was laughing as she cranked tape around the broken cot leg.

Rae took pictures often, the photos printed and tacked up on the white expanse of new drywall in a picture board—candid photos of Rae, Jodi, and Mini Wheats. Sometimes of Harper, newly single, now living in the suite of her house and paying rent to Evan—but never in toonies. Sometimes of Jodi's mother, who had been delighted with Rae, despite them not being her Zumba teacher. Sometimes of Alpine, who had eventually come around—Jodi now wondered just how much MatthewMysteryBox had to do with it.

But mostly the photos were of Jodi. Always at her best.

The End